To all H
of Beech

Crime is a Killer

BARRY HILLIER

I hope you all enjoy
my second novel
Best wishes

Barry

Barry Hillier

Fictional content

There are many districts, locations, buildings and roads in Bristol and the South West England named in this novel. Some are fictional, many exist and have been used only to fabricate a fictional story.

Crime is a Killer

FOREWARD

It was lockdown Britain once again; a second wave of the pandemic had become widespread. A good opportunity to write a second novel, I thought, following the success of my first book, 'Nightmares at Ye Olde Elm Tree'.

Whereas 'Nightmares' was a supernatural thriller, for my second novel, I wanted to create a very different story. A crime thriller perhaps; so, I contrived seven convicts, who became acquaintances in prison, all from different backgrounds, all in prison for contrasting crimes. The seven men would go on a criminal adventure together, although at the time, that adventure had yet to eventuate.

I created a businessman character, in prison for fraud. I had in mind Yosef Villin to be the brains and architect of the crimes that were about to unfold. I was explaining to my friend Derek in the gym one day, what I was devising.

'I hope you are going to include in your book a bent copper,' he remarked.

I liked that idea, so I created ex-policeman, Dillon Kelleher. Imprisoned, and discharged from the force, Kelleher was an informant to the head of a drugs cartel. I then created drug lord Stefan Bonanno, who would squeal on Kelleher, to save his own skin. That would result in the ex-copper seeking revenge on Bonanno, and convincing his prison inmates to join forces with him. With Kelleher now the prime architect of criminal strategy, the story would evolve.

I hope you enjoy this novel; my family loved it.

Barry Hillier

Crime is a Killer

CHAPTER 1

Joe Billings Junior was a son of a labourer at Avonmouth Docks in Bristol. One of five siblings, Joe's family lived in a terraced house in Clevedon, Bristol. Joe is currently serving his second sentence in Her Majesty's Prison, for burglary. His first sentence was for six months, following a raid on a petrol station. Joe is currently serving a two-year sentence; convicted for a hit and run burglary in an off licence. Joe had an accomplice that day, who caused a diversion in the shop. Unfortunately, the shopkeeper dashed to the door to head off Joe, and took a blow to his head. Joe was charged with attempted burglary and grievous bodily harm.

Joe's nickname from his schooldays was Buster Billings. He had quite a misspent youth, highly influenced by a close friend; gang-leader Teddy Granger. There were six boys in the Teddy Granger gang. They were renowned for trouble making; petty theft, vandalism, bullying. Teddy is also currently in prison, in Turkey, following a rumpus with locals whilst on holiday.

Buster, as he prefers to be called, is awaiting parole. Keen to be released, he is madly jealous of his girlfriend Chelsea. Buster and Chelsea had shared a flat in St Pauls, Bristol for approximately one year, before serving his sentence. Chelsea is a very attractive young lady, who works as a dancer in a sleazy bar in the city centre. Buster, when alone in his prison cell, cannot help but worry about her. It isn't Chelsea that he mistrusts, it is men in general. Chelsea tries to visit Buster each week in HMP; she always draws attention amongst the inmates.

Max Currigan shared a meal table with Buster and five other prisoners. Soon to be paroled, Max is serving time for illegal possession of a firearm, threatening with an offensive weapon in a public place with an intent to endanger lives.

Max was arrested at a demonstration in the centre of Bristol. Max had a loaded firearm, which he professedly claimed, he had no intention to use. He purely wanted to scare a few demonstrators. He was subsequently arrested and charged.

Max is very experienced with firearms, from serving in the Armed Forces. Sadly, Max received a dishonourable discharge from the Army, following a confrontation with a fellow soldier, whom he shot in the foot.

The oldest member of the meal table is Yosef Villin. An entrepreneur Hebrew businessman. He owns, and had shares in a total of thirteen companies registered with Companies House. Yosef was serving time for tax evasion on a further company, which he owned outright; Kohen and Rothstein Financial Services, which had been trading for five years without HMRC registration.

At mealtimes Yosef was the story teller. His tales often captured the attention of his inmates. Tales of crimes committed, such as embezzlement; a bank clerk who had pocketed deposits; a payroll clerk who didn't deposit the correct amount of VAT. Yosef told one tale of a heist at a jeweller, that prompted much softly spoken discussion amongst the group that day. Yosef was soon to be released from HMP, having served his allotted time.

Crime is a Killer

Connor Jackson was a member of the 'Fast and Furious Gang'; a group of four men, in their early to late twenties who got kicks out of stealing fast cars and racing them. Connor was serving a short sentence for an evening of sheer ludicrousness. He stole a BMW 7 series from Gordano Services near Bristol, and sped down the M5 motorway, foot down in the third lane, until another vehicle obstructed him, to which Connor would meander across lanes. He was driving recklessly and was soon reported to the emergency services. A police chase followed which eventually exited the motorway at the Weston-super-Mare junction. The Road Policing Unit (RPU) quickly pulled resources together from the local areas; traffic enforcers were positioned strategically, blocking the entrances of local villages and towns, to divert the BMW along country roads.

A PROSpike strip was used to impede or stop the vehicle that night. It proved effective; Connor and the punctured BMW crashed through a wooden fence and came to a halt in a freshly ploughed field. The M5 traffic officers reported Connor reaching speeds of up to 150 m.p.h.

Connor liked to brag about his driving escapades at the dinner table. Buster and Max were fed up with Connor's boasting; on the other hand, Yosef believed Connor would make an excellent get-away driver, if called upon.

Lonut Coltescu, born in Biertan, Transylvania, came to the UK at the age of eighteen, to work on a hop farm in Worcestershire. For several years he shared a caravan on the farm with several of the other workers. He never returned to his home country. Three workers; Lonut (who has a nickname of Donut), Alexandru and Patrin, moved south and rented a caravan at a site in Avonmouth. They moved to the Bristol area to work for a local demolition company, which was far more remunerative. Donut was a quick learner, and before very long, became one of the company's explosive experts. He continued to pay his share of the rent on the caravan whilst serving in HMP; without that roof over his head, he could be potentially homeless.

Donut was serving a sentence for aiding and abetting to a heist in a departmental store. The raid took place at night; Donut's assignment was to dysfunction the store lifts, to make them inoperable during the heist, which made him an accessory to the crime.

Donut's understanding of the English language was very good, however sometimes, he was shy of speaking English which resulted in him being one of the quieter members of the meal table.

Head of the meal table, and quite understandably so, was a mountain of a man, Niles Easter. Six feet seven, twenty-two stone, Niles would try and visit the gym most days. Born from Afro/American parents, Niles was not local to the Bristol area, unlike his meal-time acquaintances, he was from north London. Due to his large frame, Niles was very employable as a bodyguard, and nightclub doorman. He was serving a short sentence, his first sentence, for attacking a security guard, pinning him to the floor and stealing his cash box. The guard, as he hit the ground, grabbed his container of pepper spray; Niles smashed the guard's wrist to the floor, and threw the pepper spray under the security vehicle. The guard had pressed his panic button, which alerted a second guard. He jumped out of the vehicle, and faced up to Niles; he did not try to detain him or arrest him. The gigantic figure of Niles walked quickly away from the scene, turned the first corner, stepped into his parked car and drove off. A bystander recognised Niles and remained at the scene to help the police with their enquiries. Niles was also captured on a nearby CCTV camera.

Niles listened tentatively to his fellow inmates' stories of Bristol and the surrounding area. Maybe he would like to live there when he is released from HMP. Niles would love to move away from London; there are several territorial gangs in the district where he lives, with his girlfriend Makena. Despite his size, it is the increase of knife crime that worries Niles. Just before Niles started his sentence there were three stabbings in his local district. There was another doorman, a good friend, at the club where Niles worked, was stabbed five times on one of Niles' nights off. He survived; he was lucky.

Detective Inspector Dillon Kelleher had been discharged from the police force for money laundering. He was assisting the head of the drugs cartel in the south west. Dillon supplied information to Stefan Bonanno on the movement of drugs, and drug squad operations, in the local region; in return, he was paid very lucratively. Stefan was convicted for prolific drug offences. To reduce his sentence, he squealed on his informant DI Kelleher. The ex-detective's court conviction case seemed a prolonged affair. He turned to drink. His girlfriend Valesca had moved out of his house in Clifton, Bristol. She had been struggling with his drinking, mood swings and violent behaviour.

One evening, DI Kelleher had been frequenting his local, he was over the alcohol limit to drive. As he drove home, he failed to notice a prostitute on the roadside and hit her.

What resulted was a hit and run. One of her friends, another prostitute, saw what had happened, recognised the DI as the driver, and noted the last three letters of his personalised number plate. As a result, DI Kelleher was serving his second prison sentence; this time, for dangerous driving, leaving the scene of the accident, plus he was also over the limit when police officers called at his house over one hour later and breathalysed him.

Dillon also had a nickname, of Marshal. Named after a television character, Marshal Dillon, from a dated cowboy programme called Gunsmoke. His inmates only knew him as Marshal.

Quite often over the meal table, Stefan Bonanno was the subject of conversation. Marshal hated him with a passion. He wanted to get even with him, big time, for grassing on him being the source of information on drug squad movement.

'When I get out of here, I am going to fix Stefan Bonanno, good and proper' claimed Marshal.

'How are you going to do that?' asked Connor.

'I will think of a way' came his reply.

Yosef rounded off the conversation, 'I'm sure I speak on behalf of the men around this table; but if there is anything we can do to help you get even with that immoral drug dealer, just ask; we will be there for you Marshal.'

Everyone around the table nodded, gesturing their approval. Marshal smiled.

CHAPTER 2

SIX MONTHS LATER.

Following his release from prison, Buster had moved back into his flat with girlfriend Chelsea. Buster was unable to get work, so he resulted to burglary again. He had successfully stolen from a second-hand car sales yard, and two private properties. This proved slim pickings for Buster, as at one of the private houses he stole jewellery. He had no real outlets to help him shift that type of stolen goods, so he hid them in the flat. This made Chelsea very anxious. She believed she could be named as an accessory to the crime.

Buster started to spend more time in the bar where Chelsea worked as a dancer. He enjoyed watching her work; that was where he met Chelsea in the first instance. He did try to dictate how she would react though, to private dancing. That she should not ask punters outright; only if they approached her. This started to infuriate Chelsea. She threatened Buster, that if he didn't find a day job, she would kick him out of the flat. She also banished him from visiting the bar where she worked. Buster contemplated how he could get rich quick, from crime.

After his release from prison, Max moved back into his family home with his wife Eleanor and his five-year old son Drew. They lived in a semi-detached house close to Narroways Hill railway junction.

Max managed to get work at a clay pigeon shooting site, at the Bristol Activity Centre. The pay wasn't great, but it was a job. It was also an opportunity to keep his hand in, as a marksman. He practiced shooting every day, he was obsessed with guns. Max was also contemplating the 'bigger picture.' What could he do to make himself a fortune?

After his release, Yosef returned to his family home, a six-bedroom property on the edge of Woodlands Golf and Country Club, Bristol. Yosef loved playing golf; he would try and play at least three times a week. This prestigious club had a policy that amused Yosef; members had to have Hedgehog Wheels for their golf trollies; normal wheels were not permitted. Yosef's wife Leah threw a banquet for him upon his release, over one hundred guests. Yosef and Leah had three children; a son, twenty, at university; two daughters, seventeen and fifteen, one at college and one at private school.

Yosef had a lot on his mind following his release from prison. Three of his companies were experiencing a loss in profit. Kohen and Rothstein Financial Services were yet to pay their tax backlog to the Inland Revenue. The biggest worry for Yosef though, was a tragic accident to one of his financial directors. Returning home to his summer house at Hayling Island, his Mercedes veered off the road, through a barrier. He was pronounced dead. The vehicle's brakes had clearly been tampered with, reported the police.

After his release from prison, Connor Jackson moved back into his parent's home in Totterdown, Bristol. The Fast and Furious Gang had disbanded, following Connor's imprisonment. Another member of the group, Travis, had also been caught stealing and racing a Mercedes. He too was serving time. Connor was relieved, he didn't want to get in trouble again. Thanks to pressing work by Connor's probation officer, Connor was offered three days a week driving for a parcel delivery company. Connor's father put up the money to buy him a delivery van, on the proviso that Connor repaid his father.

Lonut (Donut) Coltescu moved back into his rented caravan in Avonmouth, which he shared with Alexandru and Patrin. He was able to step straight back into his old job at the demolition company. He soon found out that Alexandru had pulled a few strings for him to get his old job back, offering favours in kind with a previous group foreman.

One week after starting back at the demolition company, Donut was given a task of working with explosives again. In an old shipyard was a paymaster's building. In a back room was an extremely large metal safe. The site foreman declared the safe too heavy and cumbersome to try and move or break up. Blow it to bits Donut, was his recommendation. Donut laughed; this would be fun he thought.

Niles Easter soon slotted into his previous employment after leaving HMP. Along with another heavy, he was a bodyguard for a female television broadcaster; he also worked at the Blue Danube club, north London, as a doorman / bouncer. It was only his second night's work at the club, when he heard on his walkie-talkie, a fight had started in the bar upstairs. Niles rushed upstairs with another bouncer. His colleague stepped in between them and grabbed one of the offenders to detain him. Niles grabbed the other fighter, when he was stabbed in his side. Reactively Niles broke the man's wrist. The knife dropped to the floor. Niles kicked it away. Niles then pushed the man onto the floor and held him down until the police arrived. During that time, Niles held bar towels tightly against his wound to try and limit the blood loss.

Afterwards, in the hospital A&E, Niles was joined by his girlfriend Makena. They hugged; Makena being careful not to touch her boyfriend's stitched-up wound. Niles sat in the hospital reception area waiting to be discharged. It was then Niles had made up his mind; he was possibly going to move to Bristol.

After his release, Marshal moved back into his palatial five-bedroom home in Clifton. It was lonely; almost as bad as his prison cell he thought. Marshal tried to make it up with Valesca, his ex-girlfriend. Valesca wasn't convinced that Marshal's promise to go straight, and not drink heavily, was verifiable.

Nothing was happening, work wise for Marshal. He had applied to a private detective agency, but once they sought a reference from the police, they deterred from hiring him.

Marshal started to research Stefan Bonanno, his family, his ancestry, his business contacts, where he operated, his finances, his drug dealing empire. The man was worth millions, thought Marshal. Stefan had three grown up daughters. The youngest was a model, the eldest held a position in Bonanno Holdings, one of her father's companies. The middle daughter was quite famous in the music industry. Marzia Bonanno started her career as a model, she was also the lead-singer for a rock band. She had a tremendous voice and was soon snapped up by the band Goddess of Rock. The band were currently on a six-month tour of America, Canada and South America. Marshal's eyes lit up when he read the band were soon to perform six gigs

Crime is a Killer

in the UK, from Glasgow to Bristol. Marzia Bonanno is going to be performing in Bristol, that's interesting, thought Marshal. He noted the date, which was in two months. From that moment on, Marshal started to plot and plan a way to get even with Stefan Bonanno.

One week later, each member of the prison meal table received a telephone call from Marshal. They were all asked to meet in a pub called the Bedford Arms. Marshal knew the landlord well; he was an ex-copper. They would congregate in the back room at the Bedford. Marshal put down the telephone after the sixth call, which happened to be to Niles, and smiled. They all wanted to know what the meeting was about. Marshal would only respond to each of them in a secretive way. That raised their interest even more. Marshal was pleased with the response from everyone; he was in fact, exhilarated.

Barry Hillier

CHAPTER 3

Two days later, Marshal was on a flight from the UK to Boston, USA. He had bought online, a ticket for the Goddess of Rock concert. He was particularly interested in how the band handle their equipment and logistics, so Marshal arrived in the city one day before the concert.

Marshal reached the venue two hours before the doors were due to open. He spoke to a couple of security guards at the stage door and explained how he had flown in from England, and how excited he was to see the band, especially the Goddess. They seemed quite happy that Marshal was loitering behind the club, waiting for the band to show. Approximately one hour before the concert was due to start, a grey Ford Transit 350 arrived backstage. A Ford Focus followed. In the vehicles were the three band members and a sound engineer / roadie. Marshal approached them straight away; he explained how he had travelled from England, and how thrilled he was to see the band. He produced a glossy photograph of singer Marzia and asked for the band members and roadie to autograph the photo.

'Where is Marzia?' asked Marshal, 'Do you mind if I hang around to get her autograph?'

Drummer Alex answered, 'She will be here soon. Her bodyguard has hired a limo while we have been in the States; she will arrive with him.'

'She has a bodyguard? Wow.' replied Marshal.

'Yeah, her old man pays for him and the limo; he's filthy rich.' claimed Rory, the guitarist.

Crime is a Killer

The band and the roadie went about their business, unloading the equipment and setting it up on stage. The exception was Kyle the bassist, who had stopped to smoke a cigarette. Marshal approached him and asked, 'How has the tour gone, this is the last but one gig in America I understand. The big apple next.'

It's gone fine thanks, man,' replied Kyle. 'Marzia is the real star of the show, she knocks them dead!'

'Can't wait to see her in the flesh,' proclaimed Marshal.

'Huh,' exclaimed Kyle, 'Her flesh you certainly won't see, except for when she's on stage. She's a stuck-up bitch if you ask me.'

Marshal smiled at Kyle. At that moment a black limo arrived. The bodyguard stepped out of the vehicle.

'Who's he?' asked the bodyguard, pointing at Marshal.

'Just a fan; come all the way from England,' answered Kyle, 'He's after Marzia's autograph.'

The bodyguard sized up Marshal and beckoned him over to the car.

'May I have your autograph Marzia?' asked Marshal. She took the photograph, signed it, then ran her tongue over her top lip, in a sexually suggestive manner. She then, together with her bodyguard, proceeded to walk toward the stage door.

Marshal joined the queue to enter the concert. There was a sense of excitement in Marshal. He quickly engaged in conversation with others in the queue, interrogating them on what they knew about Marzia and the band. There was a sign up 'no flash photography,' that didn't deter Marshal from taking photos on his mobile phone. He enjoyed the performance, the band were a little heavy for his liking, but very good, very professional. Marzia was sizzling on stage, seductive, alluring. She had amazing powerful vocals, she certainly lived up to her title of rock goddess.

Marshal showed an interest in the dry-ice machine used by the band. He looked the model up on his mobile phone; it was cable and battery operated. Marshal also observed that Marzia's bodyguard was within six-to-eight feet from her for most of the evening. The exception was when she visited the ladies, where he would remain outside.

By the time the hall emptied, Marzia and her bodyguard had jumped in the limo and had left the venue. Marshal didn't think it was worth hanging around to watch the band reload their equipment, so he headed off to his motel.

The Saturday soon came around, it was Marshal's meeting at the Bedford Arms. Marshal arrived two hours early. He wanted to be well prepared, but also have some spare time to catch up with his old ex-police colleague and landlord, DI Nobby Drummond.

Marshal seemed well organised with a dossier of notes and photographs. Donut was the first to arrive, with a warm double handed handshake. Connor was the last to arrive; he had skipped off work for a few hours, from delivering parcels.

Once the group were all sat down with a drink, Marshal began by passing around photographs and newspaper cuttings of Stefan Bonanno's family. He focused however on his daughter Marzia and her band Goddess of Rock.

'You have a lot of photographs of the daughter Marzia Marshal, what are you trying to tell us?' asked Yosef.

Crime is a Killer

'We are going to kidnap her,' replied Marshal.

'Kidnap!' bellowed Max, followed by a hearty laugh, 'That sounds brilliant. Can I use my weaponry?' he asked.

'We'll come to that later Max,' said Marshal, with a cheeky grin. He went on to explain to the group about the gig in Boston; six forthcoming gigs in the UK; the last but one being in Bristol. Each ex-prisoner was asked to record the date, time and venue.

The guys took a comfort break, a few ordered another drink, then Marshal summarised the responsibilities set for each one.

'Firstly, we will need a female accomplice,' defined Marshal.

'How much money are we looking for the ransom?' asked Buster.

'Good question Buster,' replied Marshal; there was a pause. 'Bonanno is worth millions, but I feel going for a million on this occasion might be over-stepping the mark, so I'm thinking £850,000. This is an odd number, and sure to mystify the police. They are bound to be involved; Bonanno is sure to squeal. That is £100,000 each, plus £100,000 for the female accomplice, plus £50,000 possible cost ceiling. A safe house rental, getaway vehicle, cat and mouse retrieval of the money afterwards.'

'Count me in Marshal,' wailed Buster, 'Count my girlfriend Chelsea in too.'

'Anybody object to Buster approaching Chelsea?' asked Marshal.

There was silence around the room. Marshal handed out brand new mobile telephones to everyone; two to Buster.

'Phone me later Buster, once you have had chance to speak to Chelsea,' responded Marshal. 'We'll use these phones to communicate during the kidnapping. Once we have the money, we will destroy the phones. Now this is where I see each of you playing a part. The toilet block at the back of the club is like a separate building, there are single locked doors to both ladies and gents, easy to break open. Buster and Chelsea will be inside the club for the concert. Afterwards when Marzia visits the ladies loo, Chelsea will follow her into the loo and alert the team, by phoning Donut.'

'What if she doesn't go to the loo?' asked Yosef.

'She will,' replied Marshal, 'I watched her every movement very carefully in Boston. She visited the ladies before the concert started, at the interval, and after the performance. We will grab her after they have performed, at the end of the night. Some punters are likely to be on their way home by then.'

Marshal continued, 'Buster you will create a diversion, they use a dry ice machine during the concert; it is both cable powered and battery powered. You should unplug the machine and set it off into the crowd.'

'What if I am recognised?' asked Buster.

'Plenty of time to work on a disguise Buster, starting with a wig to cover your receding hairline!' came the reply.

The room was suffused with laughter.

Marshal carried on, 'Niles, I see your responsibility as looking after the bodyguard. He will be outside the ladies, but I can see him leaving his post, once Buster sets off the dry ice machine. He seems a bit of an aggressive nutter if you ask me. You will also have a ticket for the concert and your job will be to detain the bodyguard, Niles.'

Niles had a smile from ear to ear when he asked, 'Is he bigger than me?'

'No,' answered Marshal, shaking his head, 'I'm not sure if I've ever met anyone bigger than you Niles.'

'What if the ladies loo is busy?' questioned Buster.

'Hopefully it won't be, but if it is, perhaps Chelsea can at least try and keep any ladies away from the back door. Chelsea should also have a disguise; change her hair colour from blonde to black, possibly.'

Marshal turned to Donut. 'Donut, your job is to use enough explosive, JUST, to blow the door open, not endanger anyone inside the toilet block.'

Donut acknowledged Marshal with a nod of the head.

'I am thinking Donut, it would be good to throw a blanket over Marzia's head, so she doesn't see anything.'

'Max,' called out Marshal, 'You and Donut will enter the ladies loo, and grab Marzia. You can threaten her with a weapon Max, but it must not be loaded. We cannot afford to have any accidents on our first job together.'

'First,' said Max, 'Are you planning more jobs for us?' he asked.

'Possibly, but let's consummate this kidnapping first,' replied Marshal. He turned to Connor, 'Connor, it seems a natural fit to ask for you to drive the getaway vehicle. We will hire a transit van; you can hire it Connor. You will use a false name; I will arrange a forged driving licence for you.'

'You can do that?' asked Connor.

'Yes, I know someone who can create one. He needn't know what I want it for.'

'Can I drive the vehicle fast? Frighten the little lady, in the back of the van,' asked Connor. Several of the group glared at Connor for that remark.

'No Connor, you will stick to the speed limit, which is thirty. You must not draw any attention to the vehicle. The getaway must run as smooth as possible.'

Marshal looked at Yosef, who had been waiting patiently to know his responsibilities. 'Finally, Yosef, we will need a safe house, in maybe the nearby Ashley or Lawrence Hill districts of Bristol. Both are within a half mile of the venue. We should try and get Marzia into hiding as quickly as possible. Do you think you can help to organise that Yosef?'

'To hire a property in the city, we will probably require a six-month deposit,' declared Yosef, 'If we are successful with the ransom, we can of course recover the money. How confident are you with this £850,000 Marshal?'

'Bonanno is stinking rich, the value is achievable. It will be the police that we will need to give the run around. Not collect the money straight away, play cat and mouse with them,' came Marshal's reply. 'I have a plan for this, but not too much information to absorb on our first meeting. I suggest we meet again within one week, how about next Saturday, here at the Bedford.'

The group all looked at each other, to ascertain others' reactions.

'I will start to look at letting properties in the desired districts,' responded Yosef. 'I will try and identify a few properties for the next meeting.'

Crime is a Killer

'One more thing Yosef,' interrupted Marshal, 'A property with an empty garage, or double garage, would be good. Maybe an integral garage, so we can smuggle Marzia into the house without being noticed. With a garage, we can hide the vehicle for as long as it takes. Any questions anybody?'

There was much shaking of the head amongst the group. They were all trying to digest what they had just heard.

Niles was the first to acknowledge the close of the meeting. He stood up and thanked Marshal for all of his investigative work.

'If this comes off Marshal, you are definitely in charge of our next operation,' announced Niles.

The group all laughed. There were a few side conversations that took place afterwards. The mood was intoxicating.

'Final word,' piped-up Marshal 'Buster, call me re-Chelsea.'

CHAPTER 4

Buster couldn't wait for Chelsea to return home from work; she was on the lunchtime shift at the bar.

The front door clicked. 'Hi Buster, I'm home,' called Chelsea.

'Coffee, chocolate biscuit?' suggested Buster.

'Hello, you are up to something Buster, to buy me chocolate biscuits. What do you want?' she asked.

'Nothing,' he replied, 'I might have something to tell you though. How was your shift today, very busy?'

Chelsea sometimes liked to play down her work at the bar with Buster.

'Na, not really, quite quiet today, a lot of hanging around,' she replied. It was in fact quite the reverse, the bar was packed with customers.

'How would you like to earn some real cash for one night's work?' he asked.

'Oh yeah, I had forgotten, you met up with all your old prison reprobates earlier, didn't you?' responded Chelsea, 'I'm not doing anything illegal Buster.'

'This won't be illegal,' he replied. 'How would you like to earn yourself one-hundred grand, in one night.'

'Are we going to rob a bank or something?' came the reply.

'Or something,' said Buster. He went on to explain about the band, the US tour, Marshal's investigative work in Boston, the UK tour and Bristol venue, date and time.

'We are going to be a couple of rock hippies, and be in the audience at their concert,' claimed Buster. 'All you have to do is, at the end of evening when the lead singer visits the loo, to phone Donut outside, to tell him she's on her way.

Crime is a Killer

Then you just follow her, into the loo. Here is a new mobile phone you can use to do that.' Buster showed Chelsea the phone.

'And for that, I get paid one-hundred grand? she contested. 'How come?'

'We are all going to get one-hundred grand from the ransom money,' claimed Buster.

'You're going to kidnap her?' screeched Chelsea.

'Yes, that's the plan. Her father is filthy rich; he's in prison at the moment on drugs charges. He runs a drugs cartel,' replied Buster. 'Oh, one thing. When you are in the loo, try and keep anyone in there away from the back door.'

Chelsea looked at Buster in anguish. 'Why the back door?' she asked.

'Donut's going to blow it open!'

'Oh my God Buster, this is crazy,' came her reply. 'Forget the coffee.' With that, Chelsea went over to the fridge, pulled out a bottle of wine, and poured herself a large glass.

There were several minutes of silence that followed, then Chelsea asked, 'What are you going to be doing, while all of this carry-on takes place?'

'Apparently, the band use a dry ice machine; Marshal wants me to set it off, to cause a diversion,' replied Buster.

Chelsea bit her bottom lip, 'What if you get recognised?' she asked.

'I will be in disguise,' said Buster with a big grin. He produced a full-on curly black wig, that he had purchased earlier from a fancy-dress shop.

Chelsea shook her head. Not only did Buster look stupid, but this whole proposition sounded bizarre.

'Oh yes, while we are on the subject of disguise; Marshal suggested you die your hair black so no one can recognise you,' blurted Buster.

'Black!' exclaimed Chelsea.

One hour passed. Buster sat down beside Chelsea. She frowned at him.

'Babe,' he said with a cautious approach, 'One-hundred grand; you in or out? I need to phone Marshal to let him know.'

'I suppose so,' confirmed Chelsea.

Buster punched the air and telephoned Marshal on his new mobile phone. He was surprised; Marshal had set up all seven of the contacts on the new phone. He confirmed, 'Chelsea is fine to play her part in the kidnapping.'

'That's good news Buster,' replied Marshal, 'Bring Chelsea's phone along next Saturday, we can set up her device with our contact numbers. Better still, bring Chelsea.'

Connor became inquisitive about the getaway route from the club, where the Goddess of Rock would be performing. He drove over there on his day off. There were two possible routes into the district of Ashley; three possible routes into the district of Lawrence Hill. Connor drove them all; one route twice. He arrived back at the club, when a bystander, an elderly gentleman, flagged him down. Connor wound down his van window.

'You look lost son; are you looking for somewhere, only I've seen you drive past here several times?'

Connor stuttered for a minute then replied, 'Yes I deliver parcels three days a week. I was looking for Lansdown Road,

Crime is a Killer

I have a parcel left over from yesterday.' Connor thought that was a clever answer; he once had a date with a young lady that lived in that road, he knew it was not too far away.

'Parcel deliveries; don't you have a satnav?' the gentleman asked.

Connor stuttered again, 'Yes, I do have one, but it's been playing up lately; I might have to buy a new one.'

The elderly gentleman gave Connor directions on how to find the road. Connor thanked him and drove off. That was embarrassing thought Connor; he hoped Marshal would never get to hear about his exchange, with a nosy old git of a neighbour, near the club.

The days seemed to fly by; it was the following Saturday and the gang had reconvened at the Bedford Arms. Buster had brought Chelsea along to the meeting. Most of the ex-inmates recognised Chelsea from prison visits.

They all ventured into the back room with a drink, and sat around a big circular table. Landlord Nobby asked if everyone was ok, before he disappeared to stock up the front bar.

Marshal started, 'I would like to welcome Chelsea to this forum. Thank you for joining us today.' Introductions were formally conducted around the table.

'Are you comfortable with the task ahead Chelsea?' asked Marshal. Chelsea acknowledged his question with several nods of the head.

'Chelsea, there is one more thing I have thought of,' claimed Marshal. 'It could prove useful to get hold of Marzia's mobile phone. We could use it to telephone the police, or whoever is the front man to the abduction. She will most likely take a handbag into the toilets with her. I noticed in Boston, Marzia used her mobile several times. She always put it back in her bag.'

'When the kidnap takes place, when Donut and Max seize the singer, perhaps you could try and grab her bag.' It's not paramount to have it, so if it isn't possible, don't worry. I plan to be in the club that night, watching everything that's going on,' relayed Marshal. 'If she doesn't take her bag to the ladies, and she leaves it back stage for instance, I will try and grab it. A good time for that might be when Buster sets off pandemonium with the dry ice machine.'

Max picked up a muslin bag from the floor and put it on the table.

'Let's go around the table, starting with you Max. What do you have there?' asked Marshal.

Max removed the bag. 'It's a Bears Bark sawed-off shotgun, twenty-gauge version, ten-inch barrel, with a hand-formed stock,' replied Max, waving the gun in the air.

Chelsea looked petrified.

'I trust that thing isn't loaded Max,' said Marshal rather sternly.

'No, of course not,' answered Max.

Marshal noticed Chelsea's alarmed expression. 'Chelsea, you weren't here last weekend; we will have this gun at the kidnapping, but don't worry, it won't be loaded. It is just there so that Marzia Bonanno can see we mean business. At some point we expect her to relay, either to her father or the police, her kidnapper was armed. I believe this will add to our muscle, when demanding the ransom.'

Crime is a Killer

Marshal asked, 'Max, have you thought of wearing some form of disguise?'

'I have actually,' answered Max, 'I thought Donut and I should wear masks. I'm happy to organise that.'

Donut shrugged his shoulders and acknowledged his approval.

Marshal addressed Yosef next. 'Yosef, have you had any luck looking at rented properties?'

'I have five property specifications in the two areas of Bristol we had identified,' replied Yosef. 'Two have integral garages. One, is a semi-detached house, in a quiet cul-de-sac. The other is detached, with a double garage, but it's on a main road. The semi is furnished; the detached is unfurnished.'

Yosef passed the specifications to Marshal.

After much deliberation, Marshal reconfirmed, 'The integral double garage would be a necessity to smuggle Marzia into the house. I prefer the detached house on the main road. More people coming and going, on a busy road. The semi, in a quiet cul-de-sac, I feel is a risk with nosy and interfering neighbours. I also don't mind it being unfurnished. I see there is an upstairs family bathroom; we could kit out the bedroom next door like a sitting room / bedroom.'

Connor piped up, 'My parents have a two-seater couch they would like to get rid of.'

'We will need to buy new furniture Connor, or second hand from a dealer, because of fingerprints and DNA,' responded Marshal.

Marshal and Yosef discussed the terms of rent; six months, three months up-front.

'Let's secure the property Yosef,' instructed Marshal. 'Let's try for immediate possession. We probably need to organise a cash deposit.'

'I can organise that,' confirmed Yosef, 'What about the furniture?'

'I'll organise the furnishings,' said Marshal, 'Buster fancy giving me a hand with this task?'

'Sweet,' said Buster, with a boyish grin.

'Good, let's start tomorrow,' said Marshal. 'Do you know Ridley's second-hand shop in Redland?' There was a nod of the head from Buster. 'Good. Let's start there, meet you there at ten?'

Marshal turned to Donut and enquired about the amount of explosive he intended to use.

'I will only need a little explosive,' responded Donut, 'I have already smuggled the materials from my workplace. I just intend to blow the lock. No one should get hurt.'

Pleased with Donut's update, Marshal turned to Connor. 'Any luck with a vehicle Connor?' he asked.

'Well, I have been looking at transit vans, like a Ford Transit Connect, or a Vauxhall Combo Cargo, you can hire for two to five days, on a daily charge,' came his reply, as he handed Marshal two vehicle specifications.

'Perfect,' claimed Marshal. 'Let's not hire it on the day of the rock concert, let's aim for the day before. When we move the vehicle out of the garage, we should do that in the middle of the night. Here is your false driving licence Connor; or rather, Sean McBurney.'

Crime is a Killer

The group were impressed with Marshal's professionalism; Chelsea looked in awe.

Marshal turned to Niles, 'Tell me big man, do you have plans to travel down from London on the day, or the day before? Only, you are welcome to stay at my house.'

'I could arrive on the Thursday or the Friday,' replied Niles, 'Makes no difference to me.'

'Okay, that's good,' Marshal pondered for a moment, 'Travel down on the Thursday, stop with me that night; if you like you could stay at the safe house with the girl, the night we capture her.'

'Hey man, I would like that very much,' came Niles reply.

Marshal produced a voice changer / enhancer.

'It changes the pitch and distorts the user's voice considerably,' declared Marshal. He demonstrated the device; the group laughed.

'When we are at the house, we should all wear gloves at all times,' said Marshal. 'It would be good if we all took turns to nursemaid Marzia. She would then get the impression she is dealing with a gang, rather than a few individuals. The band's gig before Bristol is Croydon. I am going to have Marzia and her bodyguard tailed up until our event; find out where she stays, where she dines, what she eats.'

The group looked stunned, as they watched Marshal empty his last drop of beer into his glass.

'Any questions?' he asked the group. 'We have no need to meet here again. I will be contacting you all individually by phone; and please remember, not to use your new phones to call anyone outside this group; that could trip us up with the police. So, we have just under five weeks to show day.

The priorities being; safe house, vehicle, furnishings. Good luck everybody.'

The meeting adjourned.

In the weeks that followed, Max visited the bar in central Bristol, where Chelsea worked. He went there several times. He would openly chat to Chelsea, while she went about her business. On one occasion he asked Chelsea for a private session. She said she couldn't; it was her personal policy not to be intimate with anyone that she or Buster knew well. Max became a little forceful, but Chelsea declined, and fled to a dressing room backstage. This really spooked Chelsea. How could she tell Buster, so close to the abduction?

CHAPTER 5

One week before the Goddess of Rock concert, Yosef got the keys to the safe house. The next day, Marshal and Buster drove to Bath to hire a Luton van for the day. Marshal paid a deposit to the same leasing company to pick up the long wheel-based van in five days' time.

They drove to Ridley's second-hand shop to pick up some furniture and oddments of crockery and cutlery. Marshal had known owner Gus Overton for many years. The ex-detective had negotiated hiring each piece of furniture on a weekly basis, then return them for resale.

In the large bedroom, next to the upstairs bathroom, the two men furnished it with a single bed, bedside unit, lamp, two-seater couch, small glass top dining table with two chairs, an old rug, and a wicker commode chair.

Buster questioned Marshal regarding the commode, 'Surely Marshal, Marzia is never going to use that thing, is she?'

'Who knows, she could be locked in that room for some time,' responded Marshal.

The two men then sped over to Bono's Electrical Bargains and collected a second-hand fridge, a microwave, a two-ring mini hot plate hob and a kettle.

Max had volunteered, to work on the final preparation at the house. To fit a lock on the bedroom door, locks on the bathroom and bedroom windows, and staple a white sheet to the bedroom window, enough to let light in, but limit the risk of Marzia recognising her whereabouts.

THE DAY OF THE GODDESS OF ROCK CONCERT

Niles came down in the morning to a wholesome cooked breakfast.

'Sure, does smell good Marshal,' commented Niles.

'Big day ahead of us Niles, even bigger night ahead,' claimed Marshal.

That morning, Connor was questioned by his father, 'What's the new wagon for?'

'Just helping my mate Rocky move some furniture,' came his reply.

'What's wrong with using the van I bought you?' his father asked.

'Nothing,' came the stuttered reply of Connor, 'Rocky went ahead and hired the van, I did offer mine.'

His father shrugged his shoulders and started to walk back into the house, then turned and said, 'Why isn't Rocky driving it?'

'C'mon Dad, I've got to be the driver; I'm in the infamous Fast and Furious Gang, remember?' came his reply.

'You keep to the speed limit in that thing,' instructed his father. Which happened to be the second time Connor had received that instruction.

THAT EVENING.

Connor drove his van into the club's car park. He parked close to the ladies' toilet door. It was early, the stage door was closed, there was no sign of any bouncers. He parked the vehicle facing the back wall, providing easy access to the van's back doors. Connor, Donut and Max stepped out of the cab. It was an overcast evening, but dry and warm. Donut secured the explosive compound to the toilet door.

Crime is a Killer

The trio then decided to walk to the local. Whiskey time for the two abductors, soft drink for Connor.

Marshal and Niles parked their car in the next road. They waited at the back of the club for the band to arrive.

Buster and Chelsea caught a taxi to the venue. They joined the concert queue outside the front door. Chelsea was apprehensive and fearful. Buster rather liked his girlfriend's new appearance, long black locks, whereas Chelsea thought Buster looked like a layabout, with his long curly black wig.

Yosef left home destined for the safe house. He kissed goodbye to his wife Leah.

'Are you sure this is a good idea Yosef?' she asked. 'You have never been involved in anything like this before.'

'Don't worry dear, I trust Marshal implicitly, if anyone can pull this off, Marshal can.'

The band arrived at the venue. Rory jumped out of the vehicle and banged on the stage door. The door opened and two bouncers appeared. The band, together with their roadie, started to unload all of their equipment. Marshal and Niles watched from the street.

Soon to arrive after was a silver BMW. The bodyguard was driving, Marzia was in the back of the car; they parked alongside the band's van. As they proceeded to enter the club, Marshal turned to Niles and said, 'Take a good look at the guy with her Niles, that's her bodyguard.'

'I am so looking forward to this,' remarked Niles.

'C'mon mate, let's join the queue, let's get this show on the road,' suggested Marshal.

Buster, Chelsea, Marshal and Niles watched the band setting up assiduously. The guys in the band were all in black leathers. Guitarist Rory, with long flowing black hair; bassist Kyle with long light-brown hair; drummer Alex in contrast had a number one razor cut. He already had his jacket off, exposing a grubby white vest.

Backstage, the bodyguard wore denim jeans and a shirt. Marzia wore a tight fitting, sparkling pink jumpsuit. There were many eyes on Marzia, including Buster's, she looked hot, he thought. Marshal noticed a distinct absence of flesh from her Boston gig, where she wore a low-cut top and a mini skirt.

The concert got underway with the support act, Rosita Stancombe; she played a 45-minute acoustic set. It proved to be a definite crowd warmer for the headline act, Goddess of Rock.

Rosita had nearly concluded her set when Marzia appeared from backstage and walked in the direction of the ladies' toilet. A few cheers and claps could be heard. Her bodyguard stayed very close to her, positioning himself outside the door, preventing any other ladies from entering. Marshal watched this with disquietude. He never did that in Boston, thought Marshal.

The first Goddess of Rock set got underway; the club was buzzing. The band were electrifying. The bodyguard sat on the stage in front of Marzia, watching the crowd. Marshal kept thinking he must have noticed Niles, a big hunk of a man not far from the stage.

During the break, Marzia didn't appear from backstage to visit the ladies as she did in Boston. Something else for Marshal to ponder on, and worry about.

Crime is a Killer

The Goddess of Rock started their second set to rapturous applause. The atmosphere in the club was ecstatic. They played three encores. In the last number, guitarist Rory placed his guitar between Marzia's legs; that act raised a few temperatures in the club. At the close of the show, Marzia and the band disappeared backstage. The lights came on; time for an excited audience to go home.

As the club emptied, Niles and Buster were looking at photographs on the club walls to kill time. Marshal had phoned Max to warn him that the gig had finished, although Max could see the audience dispersing into the street. Chelsea was near the ladies, messaging Donut with holding messages such as; 'Still backstage, just waiting for her to appear.'

Suddenly Marzia did appear, en route to the ladies, followed by her bodyguard. Chelsea rang Donut's mobile. That was the signal. Donut and Max jumped out of the van's cab. Connor started the engine. Chelsea quickly followed Marzia into the ladies; there was only one other lady in there at that time.

A bouncer approached Marshal, 'Time to leave now sir,' in an attempt to help clear the club.

At that minute, Buster let off the dry ice machine. There wasn't much of a crowd remaining to fire it at, so he turned the machine toward the stage, aiming it at the band, who were taking the set down. Guitarist Rory was enraged. He ran toward Buster, jumped off the stage and wrestled with him to stop the machine. The bodyguard started to run over to the stage when Niles caught him with an uppercut. He went sprawling across the floor. Marshal made a quick exit. Niles handed the dry ice machine back to Rory.

'Come on sonny,' he said to Buster as he started to lead him away, toward the exit.

Rory shouted abuse at Buster. Two bouncers tried to intervene with Niles escorting Buster out of the building. Niles felt he had no choice; he pushed one to the ground, then landed a punch on the other. Niles and Buster made a quick exit. Buster lost his wig at the club's entrance but the pair kept running; they never looked back.

Suddenly, there was a loud explosion sound from within the ladies' toilet. The door lock had been blown apart. There was a gaping hole in the door. Marzia let out a scream, so did the other girl.

'Quick let's get out of here,' said Chelsea as she wrapped her arms around the girl and led her to the exit.

The two men, wearing masks, kicked the back door wide open. Max rushed in and pointed his sawed-off shotgun at Marzia. Donut threw a blanket over her. Marzia screamed again, louder this time. The two men led her out through the door and bundled her into the back of the van. Max and Donut climbed in the back with her. Marzia never moved with Max's gun pointing in her ribs. She did shout out several times, 'Where are you taking me?' 'Why are you doing this?'

Connor drove out of the car park and drove steadily up the road, in the direction of the safe house. He was looking out for that elderly gentleman that had previously given him directions; he was relieved that he didn't see him.

The bodyguard and the two bouncers picked themselves up and together with the band members and roadie, rushed toward the ladies' toilet.

Crime is a Killer

Chelsea had grabbed Marzia's handbag and was hiding in a cubical, trembling. The guys saw the destroyed back door.

'What the hell,' bellowed Rory.

Drummer Alex noticed a closed cubicle door. 'Are you in there Marzia?' he shouted, as he banged the door.

'No, I'm not Marzia,' came Chelsea's fearful reply, 'What has happened?' she asked.

'Someone has blown a hole in the back door,' wailed Alex.

The bodyguard walked through the devastated doorway and into the car park; there were only five vehicles remaining.

It was then the bodyguard let out a scream. 'Where's Marzia? Where's Marzia?'

CHAPTER 6

Chelsea sat in the cubicle anxiously wondering what to do next. She could hear several hysterical male voices trying to comprehend what had just happened to Marzia. Chelsea suddenly realised she had two handbags; she couldn't leave the cubicle with two bags. She took Marzia's mobile phone out of her bag to hide it in her own bag. She switched it off in case it rang and wrapped it in tissue. She quietly lifted the cistern lid and placed Marzia's bag inside the cistern. It sank to the bottom. She replaced the lid very carefully, unlocked the door and walked out of the cubical.

'Is it safe?' she yelled to the band members stood in the doorway to the car park.

'There's no Marzia,' replied Alex. 'God knows where she is or what's happened to her?'

'I'm getting out of here,' responded Chelsea, 'This is crazy!'

She walked out of the ladies, across the hall, said goodnight to the door staff, walked up the road and round the corner to where Marshal's car was parked. Marshal was very relieved to see Chelsea; he flashed his car lights at her. She jumped into the back of the car with Buster.

'Everything go to plan Chelsea?' asked Marshal.

'Yes, I think so,' she replied. 'God, I need a drink. Donut and Max broke in through the door and grabbed Marzia; she let out a scream. They must have got away. The guys that came in the loo afterwards were hollering and yelling about Marzia disappearing. I have her phone; I took it from her handbag.'

'Where is her handbag?' asked Marshal.

Crime is a Killer

'It's in the toilet cistern,' uttered Chelsea.

'Probably the best place for it under the circumstances,' said Marshal. 'DNA can be destroyed in water over time; fingerprints can remain though should the police forensic team use latent print development. Let's hope they don't find it for a long, long time.'

Chelsea slumped back in the car seat, she felt distressed so Buster tried to console her. She removed the phone from her handbag.

'Marshal, can I give you Marzia's phone? Can the police trace it?' Chelsea asked.

Marshal took the phone from Chelsea. The ex-detective switched on the phone; it wasn't locked. Good news thought Marshal. He dismantled the phone by taking out the battery and sim card; he reached into his glove box, then wrapped the phone in several layers of aluminium foil and placed it into a small metal box.

'Not anymore,' said Marshal with a wry smile.

Buster, Chelsea and Niles were again, utterly impressed with Marshal's competence.

Marshal telephoned Yosef. It was good news; Connor had made it back to the safe house without encountering any problems.

'Excellent,' remarked Marshal. 'Where is Marzia now?'

'Max has locked her in the bedroom. She is a gallant and spirited young lady, she put up quite a struggle. Max and Donut had their work cut out,' reported Yosef

'Ok, can you guys keep it that way?' asked Marshal. 'I plan to drop off Buster and Chelsea at their flat, then I think I should drive Niles back to London. He's very

41

distinguishable, he really shouldn't stay in Bristol right now.'

'Understood,' replied Yosef.

Marshal started up the car and drove to the junction, turning left to drive past the club. There were two police cars in attendance, with flashing blue lights.

'Better get your head down as we drive past, big man,' suggested Marshal. Niles crouched down and looked in the opposite direction.

Club manager Ganak Makkar had watched most of the Goddess of Rock show. When it finished, he walked one hundred yards from the club to his home. His wife Prisha had cooked a supper for him.

Ganak was about to get tucked in to a dish of tarka dal and chilli cheese naan, when his mobile phone rang; it was one of the bouncers at the club. He explained what had happened to the ladies' toilet door, and how the lead singer of the band looked to have been kidnapped. He also reported that one of the band members had called the emergency services. Ganak put the phone down and asked Prisha if she could keep his supper warm; he would have to return to the club and meet with the police. Ganak was in a state of shock.

The band and the bodyguard were stood in the car park when Rory rang 999.

'They are on their way,' implied Rory.

'Hey let's ring Marzia' suggested Alex.

Rory rang her mobile, only to report it was on answer phone. 'She must have turned off her phone,' suggested the guitarist.

Crime is a Killer

'She never switches her phone off,' claimed bodyguard Adam. 'We have to start looking for her, we need to find her.'

'Calm down Adam,' responded Rory, 'The police will be here in a minute; I suspect they will want to question each one of us.'

Adam suddenly feared for his job. How would his employer Stefan Bonanno react when he finds out that Marzia has been kidnapped?

Back at the safe house, Yosef, Connor, Donut and Max had congregated in the kitchen; they were discussing what had just happened and what to do about Marzia. The singer was screaming her head off, kicking and banging on the bedroom door.

'We have to do something to shut her up,' barked Max.

Yosef went over to the fridge. By the side of the fridge was a bottle of chloroform and some folded up rags.

'Marshal has suggested we use this as an absolute last resort,' said Yosef. 'Chloroform when inhaled should make her pass out; however, it is toxic and very dangerous.'

'Let's use it on her if it's dangerous,' growled Max.

'No Max,' answered Yosef, 'Marshal would like us to administer melatonin tablets, to make her sleepy and drowsy. Two 2 milligram tablets can be crushed and mixed with a small amount of water, or taken with soft food such as yoghurt or jam. They might take an hour or two to kick in though.'

Although the house was unfurnished there was a dilapidated old sink unit remaining in the kitchen. Yosef crushed two tablets and added a little water into a glass, which he handed to Max.

Yosef opened the fridge. 'Marshal informed me that some foods contain melatonin; the intention was to try and keep Marzia drowsy. Here are some examples, fish, eggs, nuts, goji berries, milk and cherry juice.'

Max turned to Donut, 'C'mon Donut, give me a hand, let's try and get this cocktail down the pretty lady's neck.'

At that point, Connor announced his departure for home.

'I think I will try and flag a cab down and go home. My folks think I was at the Goddess of Rock concert, so they won't be expecting me home too late.'

Ganak returned to the club; he inspected the damaged door with his two bouncers. He asked one of the bouncers to stay at the club once he had spoken to the police, while he returned home to finish his supper and pack an overnight bag. He would be sleeping at the club that night, as there was money on the premises.

The lead investigative officer at the scene was Detective Inspector Marcel Blunt. Born in the Netherlands; English father, Dutch mother, grew up in Eindhoven and joined the Korps Landeliike Politiedensten from university; later on, became an officer in the Korps Nationale Politie. He moved to the UK five years ago, to join the police force in Bristol. In that time, he had progressed to detective inspector. DI Blunt interviewed the bodyguard, two bouncers, the band, the roadie, door staff and club manager. He promised Ganak to send a forensic team to the club in the morning. He made a note of Marzia's mobile phone number, and took away a few photographs of her, supplied by the band.

Crime is a Killer

He had a long conversation with bodyguard Adam regarding Stefan Bonanno; he had never met him, but he had heard of his reputation.

Back at the house, Max and Donut put on their masks. Max grabbed his sawed-off shotgun and the two men ventured upstairs to Marzia's bedroom, with the melatonin tablet solution. Max unlocked the door; sitting on the bed with her hands tied behind her back was a very angry looking Marzia.

'Why have you kidnapped me?' she growled.

'Your daddy is going to pay us a handsome amount of money for your release,' answered Max.

'He's in prison you idiots. He won't be able to access money,' retaliated Marzia.

'We'll see about that young lady,' replied Max, 'Now we need you to take a little cocktail, which will help you to stay calm and get some sleep tonight.'

'I'm not taking any cocktail, go to hell,' yelled Marzia. 'I need the bathroom.'

'You can use the chair if you like,' suggested Donut.

'I'm not using that, I need the bathroom,' came her reply, 'Now untie my hands.' She stopped for a moment.

'What's your accent?' she asked, 'Eastern European? Albanian? Romanian?'

Donut suddenly realised he should keep speaking to Marzia to a minimum.

Max placed the gun on Marzia's breast, 'You need to say a little word, a word that we teach children, if you want the bathroom,' implied Max.

'I need to go to the bathroom, please,' murmured Marzia. Her tone had changed, as she looked at the two masked men with her big pleading eyes.

Donut untied her hands and walked in front of Marzia along the landing toward the bathroom. Max followed behind her, with his gun poised.

Donut gestured to Marzia to enter the bathroom, when suddenly she kicked him in the shin and tried to push past him. Donut gave out a yell but managed to block Marzia from reaching the stairs. Max grabbed Marzia by the hair, she let out a scream. He pushed Marzia into the bathroom, where she fell flat on her face onto the bathroom floor.

'No fancy tricks young lady,' growled Max. 'Now do what you have to, we'll be outside.' Max closed the bathroom door. Marzia stood up and latched the bathroom door. She moved over to the window and tried to open it; it was fitted with a lock. Marzia swore to herself.

Marshal drove Chelsea and Buster to their flat, then headed out to the M32 and M4, to take Niles back to London. They stopped for a coffee at Membury Services. Niles was jubilant about how he rescued Buster, and laid out the bodyguard and bouncers.

'I'm just glad you are on my side, big man,' declared Marshal.

On returning to the car, Marshal took the voice changer from the boot of his car and reassembled Marzia's mobile phone. He scrolled down through her contacts; he didn't need to scroll very far before he came across Adam, bodyguard. He showed the name to Niles, who gave Marshal a big grin of approval. He rang Adam's number.

Crime is a Killer

Adam was sat in Southmead Hospital Emergency Department; he was in agony with his jaw, following Niles' uppercut.

'Hello,' he answered.

'Hello Adam, Marzia's bodyguard.' Marshal's voice was heavily disguised, almost robotic.

'Yes, this is Adam. Who is this?' he asked.

'This is the 'Getaway Gang,' we have Marzia,' came Marshal's reply. He deliberately used gang in their proposed name.

'Getaway Gang!' bellowed Adam. All eyes in the hospital turned to him. A receptionist looked indignantly at him.

'Marzia is well and no harm has come to her,' said Marshal in a calm and reassuring manner.

'If I get hold of you, you will be pushing up daisies,' declared Adam tempestuously.

'You won't be getting hold of any of us Adam, we are too smart for you,' came Marshal's reply. 'Now tell me, who is the investigative officer in the kidnapping?'

'His name is Blunt, Detective Inspector Blunt,' answered Adam.

Marshal wondered if he knew the leading officer, but couldn't place him.

'Are you in contact with this officer?' asked Marshal.

'Yes, he gave me and the band members his contact number. Why?' questioned Adam.

'Then tell him the Getaway Gang require £850,000 from Stefan Bonanno,' instructed Marshal, 'I repeat, £850,000.' Then he abruptly hung up the phone.

Adam listened to the dialling tone on his mobile for many seconds, his thoughts were incoherent, discursive.

Marshal took Marzia's phone apart once more and placed it in the small steel box. He looked at Niles with a contemptuous smile. Niles looked at Marshal with sheer admiration.

'Let's get you back to London big man,' said Marshal.

Bodyguard Adam desperately searched for DI Blunt's card; he couldn't find it. I had better call Alex in the band, he thought, as he remembered Alex taking a card, when he suddenly found the card in an inside jacket pocket. He rang the Station.

DI Marcel Blunt had a small team to help him follow up on the abduction of Marzia Bonanno; Detective Sergeant Bryce Welles and Detective Constable Lissy Durden. It was DC Durden that answered the call from Adam.

'Hello, Detective Constable Durden speaking, how can I help you?'

'Is Detective Blunt available? I need to speak to him urgently,' declared Adam in an anxious manner.

'He isn't in the office at the moment, I can get a message to him. Who is calling please?' asked DC Durden.

'It's Marzia Bonanno's bodyguard Adam, I've just had a call from Marzia's mobile phone, demanding a ransom.'

'Ok Adam, I will call DI Blunt straight away. Did the caller state the ransom value?' asked the DC.

'Yes, £850,000.' came his reply.

Crime is a Killer

'Right Adam, thank you, can you be reached on the telephone number you are calling from?' she asked, 'In case the inspector needs to talk to you.'

His answer was yes. DC Durden rang DI Blunt with the information she had received.

'Let's put a trace on the call Lissy,' instructed DI Blunt, 'The media will soon learn about the abduction,'

'Yes Boss, it's already on social media sir,' came her reply, 'The band members have been messaging on Twitter and the band's Facebook site. Responses have been pouring in from their fan base.'

DI Blunt ended the call, with a grimacing look on his face. He telephoned Adam to hear his representation of the abductor's conversation, first hand.

Back at Chelsea and Buster's flat, Chelsea was worried sick about Marzia's handbag in the ladies' loo cistern.

'Buster do you love me?' she asked with a fearful look.

'Yes of course I do,' came his reply.

'You are a burglar, and a good one at that. Would you go back to the club and rescue that handbag for me?' Chelsea gripped Buster's hand.

After a few seconds silence, Buster agreed to return to the club for Chelsea. He would drive over there, around 1am.

Back at the house, Marzia was still locked in the bathroom. She sat on the side of the bath, tears rolling down her face. Max, Yosef and Donut were discussing what action to take next.

'I'm going to have to break the bathroom door open. I think I should fire a bullet or two at the lock,' declared Max.

'I'm not sure Marshal would approve of that,' placated Yosef.

Max decided it was time for him to act; he loaded the gun and walked up the stairs. Donut followed him.

'Open the door young lady or I'm going to blast it open,' shouted Max.

He fired two shots into the wooden door.

Marzia came to her senses and shouted, 'Don't shoot, don't shoot, I'll open the door.'

Marzia unlatched the bathroom door and stepped onto the landing. She was shaking. Donut led her by the arm back into the bedroom and sat her down on the couch.

She looked at the cocktail on the small dining table.

'I'm not taking that,' she said pointing at the glass.

Max suddenly produced a rag that had been soaked in chloroform. He smothered her face with it. Max made sure that it was administered gradually to avoid shock. Marzia slumped back on the bed, unconscious.

At 1am in the morning, Buster drove over to the club. He parked around the corner where Marshal had parked earlier and put on a pair of latex gloves. He walked quietly into the car park. The damaged toilet door remained open; the building was in darkness. He crept slowly toward the exit door to the hall, opened it gradually and shone his torch into the hall. Lying on a makeshift bed of cushions was club manager Ganak. He was snoring. Seeing him made Buster jump; he wasn't expecting anyone to be there. Ganak stirred. Buster felt a lump in his throat. He turned off his torch and slowly closed the door to the hall. His heart was pounding. A few minutes passed. Buster crept over to the cubicle that Chelsea had indicated the handbag was hidden; quietly lifting the cistern lid, he removed Marzia's handbag. He left the club without haste. If only Buster had realised there was money on the premises, the outcome might have been very different.

At 3am Marshal arrived at the house; he parked his vehicle in the next road. Yosef, Donut and Max had waited for him. Max explained the sequence of events with Marzia; Marshal inspected the bathroom door.

'What ammunition did you use?' he asked Max.

'Slugs,' replied Max.

'The door is quite damaged, firing from short range Max,' analysed Marshal, 'The spread of the pellets is quite widespread. We will have to destroy this door before we leave this house. The police may be able to trace the ammunition marks back to the gun used. I suggest we burn it when the time is right.'

The next morning, Stefan Bonanno had received word that his daughter Marzia had been kidnapped. He paid one of the guards to use his firestick tablet. He read through the many comments on the band's Facebook page. He read the band's declaration of what happened on their website. He checked the Bristol Post website; nothing posted yet about Marzia's disappearance, only a photograph and short report on the Goddess of Rock concert. Stefan studied the photograph; he thought Marzia looked incredible in her glitzy pink jumpsuit.

'Whoever has taken her had better not harm her,' he said to himself.

At that moment a guard appeared in his cell doorway. 'You have a visitor Stefan,' said the guard, 'It's the police.'

The guard escorted Stefan Bonanno to the visitors' hall. It wasn't visiting time, so the hall was empty; just DI Blunt sitting in the middle of the hall.

DI Blunt introduced himself and the two men sat down together; two guards stood against the side wall. The inspector took out his notebook and recapped on his discussions with the club manager, bouncers, the band, and Marzia's bodyguard.

Stefan spluttered, 'Bodyguard! I pay him good money to look after Marzia; fat use he proved to be last night.'

'The so-called Getaway Gang had very cleverly worked out when and where Marzia would be separated from her bodyguard,' deduced DI Blunt. He went on to say, 'The bodyguard took a call from Marzia's mobile phone. We have traced the call; it was made from Membury services on the M4 motorway.'

'So, do you think whoever has taken Marzia, has taken her well away from Bristol?' asked Stefan.

'Too early to tell yet,' replied the Inspector, 'The next call may provide us with a better indication. They did tell the bodyguard how much ransom they want for Marzia; which seems a bit of an odd amount. It's £850,000.'

'How much!' yelled Stefan. He suddenly stood up and banged his fists on the table, 'Where are we going to get that amount of money?' he hollered.

The guards started to move towards Stefan. DI Blunt indicated to the guards that everything was okay, with a wave of his hand.

'Sit down please Stefan,' shouted one of the guards. Stefan sat down again.

'Don't worry Mr Bonanno, we aim to nail this gang and retrieve the ransom,' said the Inspector in a calm and calculated way.

'I need to know that no harm has come to Marzia,' pleaded Stefan in a more dulcet tone.

'That is our priority too Mr Bonanno,' replied the Inspector. Di Blunt tore a piece of paper from his notebook and handed it to Stefan Bonanno.

'On here is a sort code and bank account number for the Avon and Somerset Police, that we intend to use for the transfer of the ransom money. It would be pertinent for you to look into transferring the requested amount of money as soon as possible. The prison guards are aware of how serious this situation is, and plan to be as helpful as they can with telephone calls etc.'

DI Blunt stood up and promised to be in touch with Stefan Bonanno as soon as possible. He bid him goodbye and left.

Stefan Bonanno didn't move; he was stunned, speechless.

CHAPTER 7

Detective Inspector Blunt returned to the station to meet with Detective Sergeant Welles and Detective Constable Durden. They discussed what to say to the various newsfeed channels and social media.

'I would like to request that the two brunette ladies who were at the scene of the kidnapping, please come forward to help the police with their enquiries,' stated DI Blunt.

'Shall I forward that request to all newsfeeds and social media?' asked DC Durden.

'Yes please,' replied the Inspector, 'Furthermore, if any of the attendees at the rock concert, or the general public, saw anything unusual at the club that night during the performance, after the performance, or outside the club afterwards, the police would love to hear from them.'

'Boss, I have set up and tested the police talk central contact centre, with voice translation, predictive dial, conversation recorder and tracking, word and phrase identification, on the office telephone,' declared DS Welles.

'Excellent, thank you Bryce,' acknowledged the Inspector. 'Lissy, if we could emphasise to the newsfeeds for the kidnappers to please call this number; we need to be satisfied that Marzia Bonanno is safe and well. In fact, we would love to hear from Marzia herself.'

DI Blunt started a storyboard in the office, with the photographs supplied by the band of Marzia Bonanno.

'I have arranged for the band and the bodyguard to come to the station at midday,' announced DI Blunt. 'Bryce, can we set up a session with either Dale or Carole, the composite sketch artists, with the band and the bodyguard? See if they can best describe the big fella that punched the bodyguard and floored the two club bouncers. If we could get a reconstructed facial composite drawing to the media by this evening, that would be brilliant. There was also this public nuisance guy that set off the ice machine, maybe we could get a sketch done of him too?'

'Sure thing, Boss,' answered DS Welles.

'One more thing,' requested the Inspector. 'Lissy, can we contact the mobile phone companies to try and trace mobile phone numbers that made calls at the club's facility, around the end of the band gig, and afterwards? Let's see if we can pick up on any commonality of calls made.'

'Will do, Boss' answered DC Durden.

'Great, thanks, I'm just going to run over to the club; they have one CCTV camera positioned at the front door; it's designed to capture people entering the club. I need to retrieve the film from last night,' announced the Inspector.

Chelsea fell asleep, waiting for Buster to return from the club in the early hours of the morning. Buster climbed into bed trying not to disturb her. Chelsea woke in the morning and caught sight of something hanging from a bedroom wall light. It was Marzia's handbag. Chelsea let out a screech and decided to plant a big kiss on Buster. That woke him.

'Buster, thank you for retrieving the handbag. Did anybody see you?' she asked.

Buster rolled over, still half asleep, 'Actually, there was someone sleeping on a pile of cushions just outside the ladies; he gave me quite a fright.'

Buster and Chelsea had a busy day ahead of them. Chelsea was tasked with buying clothes and underwear for Marzia to get changed into. It was their turn to babysit Marzia. Buster was looking forward to it; Chelsea was extremely nervous.

'What shall we do with Marzia's handbag Buster? We can't keep it at the flat,' asked Chelsea.

'I will take it over to Marshal's house later; we are going to have a bonfire. Marshal has a garden incinerator,' responded Buster.

When they reached the house, Chelsea put on a mask and Buster wore a balaclava. Yosef explained how to administer the melatonin cocktail. They weren't expecting any problems; Marzia was semiconscious. Yosef had to send his apologies; it was the funeral of his finance director later that day, at Hayling Island.

Chelsea received a text while she was at the house; it was from Max. 'See you tonight,' it said. Chelsea was on her shift at the bar that night.

DI Blunt arrived at the club that morning to meet manager Ganak Makkar.

'Good morning Mr Makkar, did you end up sleeping at the club last night as planned?' enquired the Inspector.

'Yes Inspector, I did. I didn't sleep very well though, I kept hearing noises,' came his reply.

'I can imagine, your subconscious would have been reliving many of the events from yesterday evening,' construed the Inspector. 'I've actually come back to the club to retrieve the CCTV recording from last night.'

Crime is a Killer

Ganak's facial expression became sadly fearful. 'I'm afraid, Inspector, the CCTV camera is currently broken. It hasn't been working for several months. We intended to get it repaired; we were considering the cost.'

DI Blunt was livid, 'This I find most upsetting Mr Makkar. CCTV footage could have proved invaluable to our enquiries. You must let us know which company you use for the club's insurance; they should be made aware that your due diligence on security standards has dropped off.' There was a hint of sarcasm in the Inspector's tone.

Ganak Makkar sincerely apologised to the officer.

All eight abductors watched the six-o-clock news that evening. DI Blunt was interviewed; he requested that the two brunette ladies that witnessed the kidnapping, please come forward. They showed artist caricature sketches of both Niles and Buster; the sketch of Niles made him look gruesome. There were two sketches of Buster; one with his wig on and one without.

'That's quite a good likeness Buster,' said Chelsea alarmingly.

DI Blunt called for any further witnesses to come forward that were at the club that night; that might have seen any vehicle leaving the club that looked at all suspicious. He announced the station telephone number for callers to ring. He pleaded with Marzia's kidnappers to please call that number. DI Blunt requested to know that no harm would have come to Marzia.

Connor had his television on in his bedroom. His father ventured upstairs and noticed that Connor had been watching the news.

'That's not like you to watch the news,' claimed his father, 'Did you see that the singer of that band you went to see last night was kidnapped?'

'Yes, I did see that,' stuttered Connor.

'Did you not see anything suspicious?' asked his father.

'No Dad, I left at the end of the show, I didn't see anything.' Connor thought afterwards, it was a good job that his father never knew that he was sat outside in his van all evening.

Chelsea did not feel up to working that evening after watching the news, so she telephoned in sick; she would also avoid seeing Max. Chelsea was in her kitchen when her mobile phone lit up. Fortunately, she had set it on silent, as it was Max calling.

'Why are you calling me at home?' she asked, moving swiftly into the bedroom away from Buster's hearing.

'I am at the bar,' said Max, 'Why are you not working? I thought we agreed to meet up tonight.'

'We certainly did not agree to meet,' replied Chelsea sharply, 'Please don't call me at home. I felt sick after watching the news, I couldn't have worked tonight.'

'Tomorrow then?' he asked.

'Max, leave me alone, please.' Chelsea was trembling as she hung up the phone.

The next morning, from a telephone call to the station the night before, Sophia Donald arrived at Bridewell Police Station. DS Welles greeted her and took her to a small interview room, where DI Blunt was waiting. Sophia was one of the two ladies in the ladies' toilets on the night of the abduction. She explained to the officers how there was an explosion and two masked men charged in and grabbed the singer of the band. She described how she screamed, when they threw a blanket over her and hurried her out through the damaged door.

'Do you remember what masks the abductors were wearing?' asked the Inspector.

'Yes, they were both masked up as the American president,' she replied.

DS Welles sniggered, much to the disapproval of DI Blunt.

Sophia went on to tell the officers how there was another young lady that helped to escort her out of the restroom, away from danger; how she ran for safety, but the other lady stayed in the restroom. DI Blunt thought this was curious. He asked if Sophia would spend a few minutes with a police artist to describe what she looked like. Sophia agreed to cooperate.

DI Blunt received a telephone call from HM Prison; it was Stefan Bonanno.

'Hello Inspector Blunt, it's Stefan. I have transferred some money to the police account you gave me.'

'That's good,' declared the Inspector, 'The entire £850,000 I trust.'

'No Inspector, I don't have that sort of money,' replied the prisoner, 'I have transferred £50,000.'

DI Blunt was seething. 'Mr Bonanno, I strongly urge you not to alienate this gang in any way. We want to ensure your daughter is alive and well; we also intend to recover your money. We have run a check on your bank accounts, at home and abroad, your holdings and shares; we are well aware you can access the ransom value. Surely you hold a greater value to your daughter's life?'

'I am not happy Inspector, that you investigate my opulence in this way. I am not the criminal in this instance, I am the victim,' retaliated Stefan Bonanno.

'We had no choice Mr Bonanno; we had to check how vulnerable we both would be with the ransom demands,' replied the Inspector, 'It appears to be a good job that we did. We were not expecting the short-change manoeuvre you have just instigated.'

Stefan Bonanno bid DI Blunt good day and hung up the telephone; promising to investigate further funding toward the ransom.

That afternoon, Marshal rounded up Donut and Connor and returned to the house. He went through the log that the gang had organised; Marzia had been fed several cocktails but she had not eaten anything.

'It's time for another cocktail,' declared Marshal, 'We should try and get Marzia to eat something too. Tomorrow we will need to drive her, somewhere between Membury and Leigh Delamare Services. She will need to talk to the police herself, and let them know she has not been harmed in any way.'

Marshal drove to Leigh Delamare Services on the M4 motorway. From his car, using the voice changer, he called the station's number given over on the police interview.

In a robotic voice, 'Hello, is that Detective Inspector Blunt?'

Crime is a Killer

DC Durden answered the call; she waved frantically at the Inspector.

'Boss, it's the kidnapper on the line,' she exclaimed. She answered the caller, 'One moment sir.'

DI Blunt answered the caller; the office listened in. 'Detective Inspector Blunt here; how can I help you?'

'Marzia Bonanno is our hostage. She is well and unharmed. We need her father Stefan Bonanno to put up a ransom of £850,000. Time is of the essence. We will call you tomorrow as to where the money, in used bank notes, must be dropped.'

'Wait a minute caller,' yelled DI Blunt, 'It will take time to ascertain that value in used bank notes. You must give us adequate time. We need to hear from Marzia too, that she is as well as you say she is; we need to hear her voice.'

'Listen punk,' replied the caller, 'Marzia Bonanno does not have time on her side. Tell her father to act rapidly. Until tomorrow.'

The caller hung up. Marshal continued to wrap Marzia's phone into the small steel case; he put it in his glove box and drove back to Bristol.

The telephone trace at the station came through quite quickly.

'Boss, I can confirm the call was made from Marzia Bonanno's mobile phone, from Leigh Delamare Services on the M4,' reported DC Durden.

'Leigh Delamare, Membury Services. Where are they holding up Marzia?' questioned DI Blunt, 'Hungerford, Chippenham, Swindon?'

DS Welles approached the two officers.

'This may be nothing Boss, but we have had three telephone calls from members of the public, identifying a Bristol man in the composite sketch of the long-haired rocker. Joe Billings, all three knew him as Buster Billings. I have looked up his profile, and he has done time for burglary and assault.'

'Worth following up in the morning Sergeant; a little chat with Joe, let's check out where he is living,' suggested the Inspector.

Each member of the Getaway Gang watched the six-o-clock news again that evening. The police sketches of Niles and Buster appeared once more. Niles' girlfriend Makena watched the news with Niles. When they showed his sketched portrait on the television, Makena blurted,

'That looks a lot like you Niles!'

Niles replied quite calmly, 'Handsome brute, isn't he?'

At that point, Makena gave Niles a loving shove on the arm.

In Buster's and Chelsea's flat, the mood was more intense. Buster shook his head at the two sketches of him shown on television. Chelsea let out a squeal when a good likeness sketch of her appeared, only with dark hair.

'That's it Buster, I'm off to work. I shouldn't have let you talk me into helping with the kidnapping. I should have stuck to dancing,' scolded Chelsea.

That day, Yosef attended the funeral of Herman Freud. A distinctive financial director who had worked for Yosef for many years. They knew each other from an early age; they both attended the same school in Bristol, and both visited the Synagogue in Bannerman Road. The family, friends and colleagues from Herman's work place were all very upset. It was the tragic way he died; his vehicle's brakes being tampered with, forcing Herman to drive through a barrier.

That evening Chelsea was glad that the bar where she worked was busy. It helped her to keep her mind off of Marzia's abduction. Around 10pm she wasn't very pleased when Max showed up. She tried to keep herself busy but eventually Max collared Chelsea and persistently asked for a private dance. She finally gave in and obliged Max with several dances. She thought afterwards, she is going to have to tell Buster.

At 6.30am next morning, DI Blunt's alarm rang. He cooked scrambled eggs on toast for breakfast and went over his thoughts for the day ahead. The first call he would make, would be to Joe 'Buster' Billings Junior.

CHAPTER 8

It was 9.30am, when Detective Inspector Blunt and Detective Sergeant Welles arrived at Buster Billings' address in St Pauls, Bristol. At first, they knocked on the front door to the flat, but there was no reply.

'There is definitely someone in there Bryce, try again,' said DI Blunt.

This time Buster answered the door; he wore a horrified look when the Inspector showed him his badge.

'Joseph Billings Junior?' asked DI Blunt, 'I am Detective Inspector Blunt and this is Detective Sergeant Welles; may we ask you a few questions?'

Buster nodded but at first didn't ask the two policemen into his home.

'Could we ask you inside?' enquired the Inspector.

'Yes of course,' replied Buster, and showed the two policemen into his living room.

'What's this all about?' asked Buster.

The Inspector began 'You may have seen on the news the other evening, a female lead singer of a band playing at the Liberty Club was abducted. There was a composite sketch of a man shown on the news. Three people have come forward and identified you Joe, as that man.'

'Three people!' exclaimed Buster, 'Who were they?'

'Sorry, but we are not in a position to say who they are,' replied the Inspector, 'But we have to ask; were you at the Liberty Club to see the Goddess of Rock show on the evening of?' The Inspector gave the precise date and time.

'No,' replied Buster excitedly, 'I wasn't there.' Buster was quite accustomed to telling lies.

'Can you tell us where you were on the night in question?' asked the Inspector.

There was a pause for Buster to construe his answer, 'Yes, I was home for a while, then I went into the city to see my girlfriend, who works as a dancer in a bar.'

'May we ask who your girlfriend is, and the name of the bar,' questioned the Inspector.

'Yes of course, my girlfriend is Chelsea Lewandowski, she works at the Megalodon. She's in bed right now, didn't get home until 3am last night.'

DI Blunt scribed Chelsea's details into his note book. DS Welles jumped up from the settee, and picked up a photograph of Buster and Chelsea.

'Is this your girlfriend Joe?' asked the Sergeant.

'Yes, that's Chelsea,' came the reply.

The DS showed the DI the photograph; she was blonde.

'Joe, can anybody vouch for you being at the Megalodon on the night in question?' asked the Inspector.

'Yes, Chelsea will vouch for me,' came his cunning reply.

The Inspector smiled. He wanted to quiz Buster on his attempts to get work, following his release from prison, but he decided to check that independently through Buster's probation officer. The two policemen thanked Buster, and left. Buster was relieved. He crept into the bedroom where Chelsea was still asleep; she would have to give him an alibi. Buster waited for the policemen to drive off, and telephoned Marshal. Marshal went over the details of Buster's encounter with the police, and reassured him everything seems acceptable, providing he could establish a few alibis.

DI Blunt, on returning to the police car, made a telephone call to private detective Aaron Loughty. The Inspector's department were not in a position to resource more police staff on this line of enquiry. They did however, have a small budget for outsourcing.

'Hello, Aaron Loughty' came the reply.

'Hi Aaron, it's Marcel Blunt here. I was wondering whether you might be able to put a tail on a suspect for me, in Bristol.'

'Yes, I can do that,' came the reply. The two men agreed to meet up. DI Blunt was determined to put a tail on Buster Billings.

Marshal picked up Connor, Donut & Max. Max had his sawed-off shotgun with him.

'Is it loaded,' asked Marshal. Max shook his head.

They drove to the house; they put masks on except Connor, who wore a balaclava, and collected Marzia.

'What's happening? Where are you taking me?' asked Marzia frantically.

'You are going to talk to the police,' said Marshal. The four kidnappers escorted the singer down the stairs, into the garage and into the parked-up van. Marzia noted the colour of the van and the first two letters of the number plate. Connor drove, Marshal sat in the cab, Max & Donut climbed in the back of the van with Marzia. The only light they had was their torches, on their mobile phones. They left Bristol and drove along the M32 and M4 motorways to Swindon.

Crime is a Killer

They parked up on a quiet road, with town gardens on one side, and a recreation ground on the other side. Marshal stepped out of the cab and opened the back door to the van. He held the voice changing device in one hand, and took a small steel case out of his jacket pocket. He opened it and unwrapped Marzia's mobile telephone. Switching it on, he waited, then called the police station. DC Durden answered the call.

'Hello, this is Detective Constable Lissy Durden together with Detective Constable Levi Dolivo; how can we help you?'

Marshal spoke through the voice changer slowly, 'This is Marzia Bonanno's kidnappers. In a moment I will pass the phone to Marzia, so you can hear she is alive and well.'

Lissy waved to Levi to join her, Levi sensed it was the kidnappers on the phone.

Marshal handed the phone to Marzia.

'That looks like my phone, it is my phone!' yelled Marzia, 'You must have stolen my handbag!'

DC Durden overheard Marzia and tried to interrupt.

'Hello Marzia, this is Detective Constable Lissy Durden here, can you hear me? Repeat, can you hear me?'

'Yes,' replied Marzia, 'I can hear you. The guy that spoke first was talking through a device; one of the guys has a gun, he shot the bathroom door when I was inside; they drove me some distance in a grey van, WU number plate,' Marzia blurted out.

At that point Donut wrestled the phone off of Marzia and handed it back to Marshal. Max struck Marzia on the side of the head with the stock of his shotgun. He drew blood.

Marshal replied to the police officer, via the voice changer, 'So officer, you have heard from Marzia, what is the situation with the £850,000?'

'Wait,' barked DC Durden, 'how can we prove it was actually Marzia? Can we ask her a few questions that only she would know the answer to?'

There was a pause. 'Fire,' instructed Marshal, 'We don't have much time.' Marshal noticed a dog walker approaching them in the distance.

'Let's ask her, her date of birth and her mother's maiden name for instance,' responded DC Durden.

Marshal asked those two questions to Marzia.

'Why should I help you?' she cried, holding her head. Max held up his gun and gestured to hit her once more. Marzia forcefully answered the two questions, which Marshal fed back to the constable.

'I'll need to run a check on that information,' declared DC Durden.

'You will have to do that in your own time,' demanded Marshal, 'Now what is happening with the money?'

'My understanding is Mr Bonanno is in the process of transferring the ransom money into a police bank account, so we may draw down the money in used notes,' answered DC Durden.

At that point Marshal closed the back door to the van, removed his mask and walked back to the cab; the dog walker was fast approaching.

'Hold the line,' hollered Marshal, and put the phone under his leg to try and muffle his conversation.

Crime is a Killer

'Connor take off your balaclava,' he whispered as the dog walker was about to walk past the parked vehicle.

The walker stared at the two men in the cab, but continued walking, much to the relief of Marshal and Connor.

When the walker was sufficiently distanced from the van, Marshal answered the telephone once again, 'Now listen Constable, this is important. Outside Bristol Parkway station, approximately twenty yards to the west of the entrance, is waste bin, next to a lamp post. Bristol City Council must guarantee that bin is completely empty when the money is dropped off there.'

'You want to put £850,000 into a waste bin?' exclaimed DC Durden.

'Correct, in and around the bin in money sacks,' answered Marshal, 'In used bank notes; the drop will be collected late at night. It would be helpful to disconnect the lamp post light at that location. This is the most important instruction; no one from the police must be anywhere near Bristol Parkway that night. All roads must be kept clear. We will be watching every move. If there are any mistakes, it will be Marzia that suffers. I will telephone again tomorrow.'

'Wait!' cried DC Durden, but it was too late; the phone line went dead.

DI Blunt met with private detective Aaron Loughty for a coffee. They discussed an ongoing hourly fee for the private detective, and reached an agreement. DI Blunt produced copies of the composite drawings of the Buster lookalike; his address, his vehicle description and licence plate number, and the club details where Chelsea danced. The private detective said he would start tailing Joe Billings that evening. They shook hands and DI Blunt returned to the station. He had been tipped off that the abductors had called.

The storyboard in the office was becoming more interesting. Four composite sketches, photographs of Marzia and Stefan Bonanno, with the following names; Joe Billings Junior, Chelsea Lewandowski and Niles Easter. There had been several telephone sightings of Niles as one of the caricatures; DI Blunt however wasn't treating this identification as a priority, as Niles Easter resided in London; he wasn't aware of the prison connection.

DI Blunt got his team together, which now included DC Dolivo. He reiterated to the two DCs, details of their conversation with Joe Billings Junior, and how he had assigned a private detective to tail him. That he intended to pay a visit to Chelsea Lewandowski at the Megalodon bar in the city centre. They listened to the recording of the kidnapper's telephone call.

'Boss, we have checked out Marzia's date of birth and mother's maiden name; it's a match. That genuinely was Marzia speaking,' reported DC Durden. 'So, we now know one of the abductors has a firearm, which he fired into a bathroom door! We checked the signal with the telephone operator; the call was made from the Old Town area in Swindon. We know they are using a grey van, and WU registration is Bristol. The pickup point is at Parkway station, in and around a waste bin.'

DI Blunt pondered for a moment; 'Let's check out with the local vehicle hire companies in Bristol for any recent grey van hire, and if so, who to? Bryce and I should take a look at this drop point. It's most unorthodox.'

Crime is a Killer

'One more thing Boss,' interrupted DC Durden, 'There were three calls made on mobile phones at the Liberty Club on the night of the abduction, owned by the same person. All three mobiles were registered to a Mr Alun Muir.'

'Interesting,' claimed DI Blunt, 'Let's do some more digging on that fact.' DI Blunt closed the session.

DI Blunt and DS Welles travelled to Bristol Parkway. The location of the bin was quite obvious to the two officers.

'£850,000 in used notes certainly won't fit into that bin, Bryce,' contemplated the Inspector, 'They asked for money sacks, in and around the bin; very unconventional.'

'Boss, there is no CCTV line of site to this bin, or along the immediate road exit, just outside the station entrance,' observed the Sergeant. 'Probably why the kidnappers have chosen this location.'

DI Blunt called the station. DC Durden answered the phone.

'Lissy, Bryce and I are at the drop off point; there is no CCTV coverage at the location. We best check with Bristol City Council on CCTV coverage on roads leading to the station from the different approaches. For example, Brierly Furlong, Church Road, Westfield Lane, Great Stoke Way, North Road and Hambrook Lane. In addition, the kidnappers requested no lamp post light. When we talk to the council the serial number is BCC155.'

'Will do Boss. We had a call from Stefan Bonanno; he said he has deposited £500,000 into our bank account,' reported DC Durden.

'What's he playing at?' questioned the Inspector, 'Thanks Lissy; I'll try and give him a call.'

Aaron Loughty pulled up outside Buster & Chelsea's flat. He looked for Buster's car but he couldn't see it. Buster had driven over to Marshal's house to dispose of Marzia's handbag.

Back at the safe house, a masked Max and Connor were there to escort Marzia to the bathroom, and try and get her to take a cocktail and eat something. She decided she wasn't going to lock herself in again. After two days without eating, Marzia was ravenous; she hadn't noticed that Max had slipped a cocktail into a glass of cherry juice. Max noticed that Marzia had ripped the sheet open at the bedroom window.

'Trying to find out your bearings by any chance, young lady,' enquired Max.

'I could see high rise buildings, a couple of churches, a tall crane, I can hear a railway; I know we are in Bristol,' she claimed as she scoffed her food. 'I know we are in Bristol; it was a short journey in that van when I was first seized.'

The two ex-convicts watched Marzia finish her drink and food, then locked her in the bedroom once more.

Buster drove over to the Megalodon and parked down the road from the bar. Aaron Loughty observed his arrival; he had also parked close by. Ten minutes later, DI Blunt arrived and entered the bar. He presented his badge to the barman and asked to speak to Chelsea Lewandowski. The barman called her over.

'That's the policeman that came to the flat this morning,' whispered Buster. Chelsea looked worried.

Crime is a Killer

'Remember Chelsea, I came to see you here the night of the kidnapping, you must tell him you were working that night,' mumbled Buster.

Chelsea joined DI Blunt and asked him if he would like a private dance.

'No thank you,' was his reply. He questioned Chelsea on her relationship with Joe Billings, where she was on the night in question, and did she know where Joe was on that evening.

'Yes,' came her answer, 'he was at home, but he came in here to see me for most of the evening.'

'Can anyone else bear witness to Joe being here other than you Chelsea?' asked the Inspector.

'Yes, Hannah can, she is another dancer here,' claimed Chelsea.

'Is she working this evening? Can I speak with her?' enquired DI Blunt.

'She isn't here tonight,' declared Chelsea, 'Wait a moment.'

Chelsea asked the barman regarding Hannah's rota. She returned to the inspector with the news that Hannah Nowak would be dancing the following evening. At that point DI Blunt thanked her for her time, and left.

Chelsea telephoned Hannah straight away and pulled in a favour. She was having a heart-to-heart discussion with Buster when the barman leaned over and murmured to Chelsea, 'You're on next luv!'

Chelsea looked over to the front door; suddenly there was Max. Max noticed Chelsea was with Buster; he teetered, pivoted, and decided not to enter the bar.

Buster didn't stay at the bar very long before he drove back to their flat. He failed to notice he was being followed.

DI Blunt had an idea about the shortfall in Stefan Bonanno's ransom money. He would have a word with his Detective Chief Superintendent in the morning.

Crime is a Killer

CHAPTER 9

At 8.30am Detective Inspector Blunt knocked on the office door of his boss, Detective Chief Superintendent Elliott Dawes-Drake.

'Good morning Governor, any chance of a chat regarding the Marzia Bonanno kidnapping?' requested DI Blunt.

'Good morning Marcel, let's get the department together for a quick briefing,' suggested DCS Dawes-Drake.

DI Blunt gathered his team in front of the storyboard. Three photographs had been added, two access roads to Bristol Parkway station and the unexpected drop point; the bin. The DCS joined them for the briefing; an interesting situation for Marcel Blunt, as he had never had a younger boss before.

DI Blunt, for the benefit of the Superintendent, covered their interview with Joe Billings Junior, Chelsea Lewandowski, and how he had put a tail on Joe Billings using a private detective. He explained how the Liberty Club had failed to use their CCTV camera on the night of the abduction, and how the drop off point at Parkway station had no CCTV coverage.

'Are there any vantage points we can watch the pick-up?' enquired DCS Dawes-Drake.

'There could be a good spot at St Michael's Church, from the graveyard,' reported DI Blunt. 'There is also the short stay car park right opposite. I suggest we have an unmarked car set up in there.'

'How soon can all this all happen?' enquired DCS Dawes-Drake. 'What's the latest situation with the ransom money?'

'Glad you asked that Guv. Stefan Bonanno has transferred £500,000, not the full amount,' reported DI Blunt, 'I thought we could offer that to the kidnappers, see if they take the bait.'

DC Durden spoke up, 'Boss, I checked with the bank's director first thing this morning; the money is in the police account, we could draw it out today if necessary.'

'Excellent,' answered DCS Dawes-Drake, 'Let's move on the half million with the kidnappers, see how they reciprocate. How many members do we believe is in this Getaway Gang?'

'It's hard to say,' answered DI Blunt, 'We believe at least six; two abductors, the driver, the girl, the big fella, the ice machine idiot.'

DC Dolivo was the next to speak up, 'Boss, on sightings from the composite drawings shown on TV, we have four different sightings of the girl, all from different locations. Eleven sightings of the long-haired rocker, four of which are Joe Billings, seven others, one in Cardiff? Thirteen sightings of the big guy; six of those named one guy, a Niles Easter, who lives in north London.'

'Thanks Levi,' responded DI Blunt, 'These artist impressions are excellent, they can lead you straight to the criminals; they can also send you up a few blind alleys.'

'Boss, I've taken the liberty to telephone the Met on the Niles Easter identifications. They have assigned a DS Parkin and DC Jha to pay a house call on Mr Easter later today,' reported DC Dolivo.

Crime is a Killer

'Good,' came the reply from DI Blunt, 'Levi, you are following up with the council on CCTV cameras I believe. Lissy, you're also talking to the council on the bin collection. We need to call in support from the Road Policing Unit. See if we can arrange an unmarked police car in the station car park. See how many cars they can provide on roads leading to Parkway; that will determine where we can place the vehicles strategically. Bryce, you're talking to forensics; see if they have turned up anything at the Liberty Club. We'll go back to the drop off point later and establish our presence there. Before we do that, I'd like to pay a visit to Stefan Bonanno in HMP. Apparently, he has drawn up a list of the top ten people who would be most likely to kidnap his daughter.'

'Who needs friends, when you have that many enemies?' remarked DS Welles.

DI Blunt looked at DCS Dawes-Drake to ascertain his acceptance to close the session. A nod of the head was sufficient.

Yosef was baby-sitting Marzia. Marshal was on route to Bath to telephone the police department. Connor, Max and Donut were busy with their day jobs. Buster was still in bed with Chelsea when he received an SOS telephone call from Yosef; Marzia needed the bathroom.

Marshal sped down the M4 motorway once more, exiting at the Bath junction. He stopped at a vantage point at a hamlet called Pennsylvania, and telephoned the police station. All the team were in the office on this occasion. It was a good opportunity for DI Blunt to hear the kidnapper first hand, and experience the robotic voice enhancer.

'Hello, this is Detective Constable Durden, how may I help you?'

'Marzia Bonanno's kidnappers here, the drop is tonight; are you ready with the money?' asked Marshal.

DI Blunt came to the telephone, 'Detective Inspector Blunt here caller. There is a slight problem; yes, we are ready with the money but we only have £500,000. Will you take half a million in exchange for Marzia?'

'I will need to consult with the rest of the Getaway Gang; I will ring you back.'

Marshal hung up. DI Blunt wanted to ask if Marzia was alive and well, but the call ended too swiftly.

'Bryce, we had better hit the road, as it looks like the drop could be on for tonight,' construed the Inspector. 'Lissy, Levi, we need to get the council to empty that bin and temporarily seal it. We also need to talk to the bank and locate the money. Plus, talk to the Advanced Security Officer and arrange for an armed team of officers and security vehicle to collect the money. Also, check with the Road Policing Unit on what cars they can provide tonight; if you need help with that, have a word with the governor.'

DI Blunt and DS Welles quickly gathered their belongings, shut down their computers and left the office to visit Stefan Bonanno.

Marshal wrapped up Marzia's mobile phone into the steel case and hid it away in his glove box. He ran some quick calculations on the money, then called each member of the Getaway Gang on his purpose bought mobile. His first call was to Yosef. 'Hi Yosef, it's Marshal; how are you, and how is Marzia?'

Crime is a Killer

'Hi Marshal, I am fine, thank you,' replied Yosef, 'Not so sure about Marzia though, as she is calling for the bathroom. I have had to get Buster out of bed to come and help.'

'Okay, good, be careful with her Yosef, don't take any chances,' deliberated Marshal. 'Now listen carefully, the drop off to Parkway could be tonight. They are offering half a million pounds. I have run a rough calculation and after expenses, each of the gang would receive in the region of £60,000. I need a yes or no in the next hour, if we are to stick it out for the full amount.'

Yosef didn't need an hour to answer. It was a yes, take it. Marshal spoke with each gang member. Seven said yes; only one thought no, and that was Marshal.

Bodyguard Adam paid a visit to Stefan Bonanno in prison; he was in fact summoned by his employer.

Adam arrived in the prison meeting room first and took a seat. He was wearing a bandage to support to his jaw. When Stefan arrived, Adam stood up and attempted to shake his hand. Stefan declined and sat down. He wore a perturbed expression. Adam followed and sat down.

'My accountant has written to you today Adam, terminating your employment as Marzia's bodyguard,' informed Stefan Bonanno. 'I have been notified by the band that the final UK gig has been cancelled.'

'Any news on Marzia, Stefan?' asked Adam.

Stefan Bonanno avoided the question. 'I heard it first hand, that whilst Marzia was in the ladies' toilet at the Liberty Club, you deserted your responsibilities and went after some lunatic that had set off an ice machine.'

'Yes sir, I did, that was the natural thing to do; he was aiming it at the band,' explained Adam. 'I had looked after Marzia extensively up until that point, especially when we were overseas; in particular when in South America and the USA.'

'You were paid handsomely,' snapped Stefan, 'Do not ever ask me for a reference; and should anything happen to Marzia, you might want to consider leaving the country.'

Stefan Bonanno stood up and walked out. Adam was stunned, dumbfounded.

Marshal drove north, over the M4 motorway, and stopped his car in the village Old Sodbury, where he unwrapped Marzia's mobile phone once more, and called the police station.

'Hello, Detective Constable Durden speaking, how may I help you caller?'

'This is the Getaway Gang. We will accept £500,000 in exchange for Marzia Bonanno. We will collect the money in used bank notes tonight. We will instruct you on this telephone number, where to find Marzia. She is and will be alive and well, providing there is no police presence at the drop off point.'

Marshal hung up.

DC Durden called DI Blunt; he was in his vehicle on route to HMP to meet Stefan Bonanno. He pulled the car over onto a grass verge.

'Boss, the kidnappers have just called, they will accept £500,000 in exchange for Marzia, and have asked for the drop off tonight,' reported DC Durden.

'Excellent, keep me informed on the bank situation,' replied DI Blunt, 'Did they say how we will get Marzia back?'

'Not exactly Boss. They said they would call the station number once they see the money, on where to locate her,' answered DC Durden. 'They stressed no police presence; should we cancel the unmarked car in the station car park?'

'No Lissy, we should go ahead with that, and the cars on the routes out of Parkway,' confirmed DI Blunt.

'One more thing Boss,' said DC Durden, 'The kidnappers' calls were made from Marzia's mobile once again. The call locations were Pennsylvania and Old Sodbury. Both villages are a few miles from Bath.'

'Thank you Lissy. They are giving us the run around,' claimed DI Blunt. 'Service stations, Swindon, now Bath. I wouldn't be surprised if Marzia Bonanno is hidden somewhere close to Bristol.'

It was just after midday, when DS Parkin and DC Jha knocked on the front door of Niles Easter's home. Niles' girlfriend Makena answered the door.

'Good afternoon,' said DS Parkin, showing his badge to Makena, 'Is Niles Easter home? May we have a word with him?'

Makena acknowledged the two officers and went indoors to fetch Niles.

'Baby, it's the police at the front door; they are asking for you, what have you done now?' asked Makena.

'Nothing,' replied Niles. When the composite police sketch first appeared on television, Niles expected to be questioned by the police; after a few days he had become more relaxed. Niles looked at the coffee table in front of him; there were property specifications of houses in Bristol. He quickly turned them upside down and put them on a lower shelf of the coffee table.

Niles greeted the officers at the front door. DS Parkin enquired if he could ask him a few questions, inside the house. Niles invited the two policemen into his sitting room. DS Parkin was five feet eight tall; Niles towered above him.

DS Parkin showed Niles the composite sketch. Niles laughed at the likeness, and pretended not to have seen it before. The Sergeant asked him on his whereabouts on the night in question. Makena had stayed in the room, so Niles felt he had to establish some truth.

'I went to stop with a friend for the weekend in Gloucester,' came Niles' reply.

The Sergeant asked him for his friend's name and address. Niles gave them a false name, and made up an address. The Sergeant recorded the information and they bid Niles and Makena good day, and left.

'Why did you lie to the police?' bawled Makena.

'Don't worry Makena,' replied Niles. 'They probably won't follow up on that. A different police force will be operating in Gloucester, so that is three separate forces on the case, including the Met and Bristol.'

Makena wasn't so sure.

Buster took another call from Yosef; could he help out with Marzia at the safe house. Marshal would be calling in later once he had telephoned the police. Buster gorged down a bowl of cereals, checked the local news channel on the television, kissed Chelsea goodbye and left the flat. Aaron

Crime is a Killer

Loughty watched Buster as he closed his front door. He threw his tabloid newspaper onto the passenger seat.

Buster drove off, to cut across the city centre to the safe house; Aaron Loughty followed him. Probably because Buster was driving over to the house, he was feeling anxious, but he was also attentive. He noticed a black Mercedes behind him and became mindful that it might be following him. Buster swung a left turn at the next junction. The Mercedes turned in the same direction. I am being followed, thought Buster. He drove toward the city centre and parked up on double yellow lines, outside a dry-cleaners. Aaron Loughty observed this but decided to drive around the block, rather than also park on double yellow lines. Buster, inside the dry-cleaners, was fumbling through his pockets looking for his ticket; he was watching out the window the entire time. The black Mercedes drove past the dry-cleaners a second time. Buster watched the car until it was out of sight.

'Sorry,' blurted Buster at the shopkeeper, 'I must have left my ticket at home.' He left the shop in haste, jumped in his car, and turned right, down an alley.

Aaron Loughty drove past the shop for a third time. Joe Billings' car had gone. He raced to the end of the road; Joe's car was nowhere to be seen. Bugger, he thought, Joe Billings had escaped from his grip.

Buster parked up in the next road to the safe house; he felt nervous and apprehensive. He telephoned Marshal and explained how he had been followed and how he had cut and run and given the driver the slip.

'Buster, park your car at least half a mile away from the house,' instructed Marshal. 'The police will know your car's description and number plate. They might radio the details around any patrol cars in the area. I will be arriving at the safe house in approximately thirty minutes.'

Buster moved the car as Marshal had requested. He walked back to the house and arrived simultaneously with Marshal.

Yosef was relieved to see them; Marzia was desperate to use the bathroom. Marshal informed Yosef on how Buster had escaped a police tail on route to the house. Yosef flung his head back in angst.

'The sooner we exchange Marzia for the ransom the better,' implied Yosef.

'The drop at Parkway is tonight,' declared Marshal.

'Yes!' hollered Buster, as he punched the air.

Crime is a Killer

CHAPTER 10

Marshal and Buster cooked Marzia bacon and tomatoes on toast, which was intended as a brunch. Buster sat on the bed and kept watch.

'How long do you think you can keep me here?' she asked. 'I'm sick of looking at you all, with those stupid masks on.'

'Not long now honey,' replied Buster. 'The drop is tonight.'

'I am not your honey; what do you mean, the drop is tonight?' retaliated Marzia.

'The police are to deliver half a million quid to our chosen location, tonight,' said Buster.

'Half a million!' she screeched. 'Is that my father's money?'

'Yes, daddy has put up the cash,' replied Buster. 'We wanted more; but half a million will do for starters.'

'Starters!' yelled Marzia, 'You are never going to get away with this; the police will catch you, and when my father finds out who you all are, you'll be sitting ducks.'

At that point Marshal joined them in the bedroom. 'I see you two are getting on famously,' observed Marshal. He picked up Marzia's empty brunch plate, and left her a large glass of cherry juice, laced with crushed melatonin tablets.

'I suggest you get some rest Marzia; if we exchange you for the money later, it could be a busy night ahead,' advised Marshal.

While all this was happening, Buster's car had been seen by two officers in a police vehicle. The cars whereabouts had been radioed back to the police station; in turn, DC Durden had telephoned Aaron Loughty with the location.

DI Blunt and DS Welles arrived at HMP. They were shown to a small interview room where they waited for Stefan Bonanno. Stefan looked haggard, exhausted.

'Have you heard from Marzia?' he asked.

'Yes, we spoke to her briefly yesterday; she came over very lively and fed us with as much information as possible, in a short space of time,' answered DI Blunt. 'We were able to run a check with her on her date of birth, and mother's maiden name; it was definitely Marzia.'

'Have you received my money?' asked Stefan.

'Yes, thank you Mr Bonanno. The indications are that the exchange will take place tonight. We will be ready for them,' assured DI Blunt.

'You had better catch those bastards! And keep my money safe,' threatened Stefan.

'Don't worry Mr Bonanno; we will have vehicles and marksmen in place to intercept the kidnappers, and the money,' guaranteed DI Blunt. 'Now, I believe you have drawn up a list of possible kidnappers, Mr Bonanno.'

Stefan Bonanno reached into his pocket, watched carefully by a prison guard, and handed the list to the Inspector.

Ten names were on the list. DI Blunt focused on the top three names; Caleb Tchaikovsky, Volker Von der Leyan and Linwood McGinn. He read the three names out to Stefan.

'Tell us Mr Bonanno, these first three names on the list, why do you suspect these gentlemen to have organised the kidnapping of Marzia?' questioned DI Blunt.

'Caleb was my business partner in Russia. I sold my majority shares in our company, the share price plummeted, Caleb lost a lot of money. He was very angry. I have received death threats from him, then I ended up in HMP,' explained Stefan. 'Volker, a similar situation in Austria; he swears he will get even with me one day. Linwood double crossed me on a deal; I had him kneecapped, his left leg.'

'Thank you, Mr Bonanno. We will try and make use of this list,' acknowledged DI Blunt.

What the Inspector could not have known at this stage; seventh on the list was Detective Inspector Dillon Kelleher (Marshal). Tenth on the list was Yosef's deceased financial director, Herman Freud. The two police officers offered their assurance once more to Stefan, and left.

Marshal and Buster were replaced at the house by Max and Donut; they were the evening shift to nursemaid Marzia. Max soon realised he would not be able to visit Chelsea that night at the Megalodon bar; think of the money for the abduction he kept telling himself.

Buster walked a half mile back to his car. He never noticed Aaron Loughty in the black Mercedes, parked close by. Buster's first stop-off was a betting shop, where he spent the next two hours, before returning to his flat for food. Aaron Loughty had followed him to both locations. Chelsea would have an alibi that evening; she was working at the Megalodon bar. Marshal had recommended that Buster visit the bar that evening, so he would also have an alibi.

Marshal caught the 15.35 train from Bristol Temple Meads to Bristol Parkway. As he left the Parkway station, he ventured into the station car park. Parked on one side was a navy-blue BMW, with two police officers stood by the side of the vehicle. They were engrossed in conversation, and hadn't seen Marshal crouch down between two parked cars. With his mobile phone he took a photograph of the two policeman and the BMW, before walking beyond the car park, toward St Michael's Church. He walked past the designated bin for the proposed drop; he noticed it hadn't been emptied. Marshal then noticed in the church grounds, two workmen removing a section of hedge, and folding back a section of chain link fence. A police officer watched over them, from behind a small stone wall, on the edge of the graveyard. Marshal flagged down a taxi to return to Temple Meads; he was conscious not to appear on CCTV returning to Parkway.

Each member of the Getaway Gang received a text from Marshal. 'Police present at Parkway. Unmarked car and stakeout in the church grounds. Will cancel the drop tonight. There is a masterplan for tomorrow night.' Each member of the gang was disappointed with the news, however they trusted Marshal to accomplish the trade-off.

From Temple Meads, Marshal called Niles. He was keen for the big man to also have an alibi for that night, and the following evening. He was aware the police might be watching his, and Buster's movements. Fortunately, Niles was working at his local bar as a doorman on both evenings.

DI Blunt returned from Parkway station, happy that preventions were in place to trap the Getaway Gang. He returned to Bridewell police station for an update with DC Durden.

'Boss, I spoke to the bank fifteen minutes ago; the money has been loaded onto the security vehicle. The used bank notes are in money sacks, as requested' reported DC Durden. 'The intention is for the vehicle to remain at the drop point; once the station is closed and the remaining staff and passengers have all departed, the armoured vehicle will be unloaded at the drop point. The vehicle will stay within reach of the money until the abductors arrive at the site, then the security vehicle will drive off, out of sight.'

'Good, excellent work Lissy,' replied DI Blunt. 'I can confirm the unmarked vehicle and armed police are in place at the station.'

'The council workers have arrived at the drop off point; they are scheduled to remove the bin contents, cover the bin, and they will disconnect a nearby lamp post, so the drop point will be in darkness,' outlined DC Durden.

'Good, let's hope the gang appreciate all of our efforts on their behalf, when we lock them all away in HMP.' DI Blunt raised a smile.

'How many vehicles were we able to secure on routes out of the station,' asked DI Blunt.

'Four,' detailed DC Durden. She went on to inform the Inspector which routes would be covered.

'Hopefully we shouldn't need any more than four. We need to make sure we have a vehicle on the East Access Road, which leads to the station car park, as well as the main roads,' confirmed DI Blunt. 'Who is on night duty? Is it Levi?'

'Yes Boss, DC Dolivo will be manning the office, and be on hand to coordinate the Marzia Bonanno exchange,' responded DC Durden.

DI Blunt announced, 'I am going to grab some food on route to the Megalodon bar; I am hoping to catch up with a dancer called Hannah Nowak, who can confirm whether Chelsea Lewandowski was working at the bar on the night of the abduction. After that, I shall stake out at St Michael's, Parkway station.'

'Good luck Boss,' replied DC Durden. 'One more thing, before you go. Do you remember four mobile phones used at the Liberty Club that belonged to the same owner; a Mr Alun Muir?'

'Yes, I remember.'

'We have traced where he acquired the phones; from a dealer in Bath. He bought twenty altogether. That's a bit odd don't you think, Boss?'

'Yes, I agree, that does sound abnormal,' replied DI Blunt, 'Better stick this Alun Muir character on the storyboard along with the dealership.'

Yosef took a call from the deceased Herman Freud's son Mattheo. He had been laboriously going through his father's paperwork files, accounts and emails. He advised Yosef that he had found a threatening email from a Stefan Bonanno, demanding a sum of money to be paid for the sale of stocks and shares.

Yosef went silent. 'Stefan Bonanno, you say; how much was the demand for?' asked Yosef.

'£195,000,' responded Mattheo. 'Should I call the police?' he asked.

'Yes, I think you should Mattheo. Try not to involve me at this stage; I can speak with them at the investigation stage,' recommended Yosef.

Yosef put the phone down; his thoughts were suddenly incoherent. Could Stefan Bonanno have anything to do with Herman's accident? He thought it would be a good idea to discuss this with Marshal in the morning, when he would have a clearer head. What Yosef did not know was that

Crime is a Killer

Herman Freud was on Stefan Bonanno's list of the most likely people who might have kidnapped Marzia.

DI Blunt paid a visit to the Megalodon bar to interview Hannah Nowak. He approached the barman to ask if Hannah was working that evening; he noticed Chelsea Lewandowski was working there that night. The barman called Hannah over; she wore an anxious, uneasy expression. DI Blunt asked her if Chelsea was with her on the night of the kidnapping; she confirmed they were both working that night. Call it detectives' intuition, but the Inspector didn't believe her. The Inspector asked the barman if he could see the staffing rota.

'We don't have one here Inspector,' responded the barman, 'You will need to contact the boss. He's Russian, he owns several bars like this one, in London.'

DI Blunt noted the contact details of the owner; this frustrated the Inspector. Despite this, he left the bar quite excited. Time to catch and arrest the Getaway Gang.

It was 9.30pm, Aaron Loughty had parked his Mercedes near Buster and Chelsea's flat. He was about to give up and go home, when Buster appeared at his front door. Buster jumped in a pre-ordered taxi. Aaron Loughty followed the cab to the Megalodon bar. He messaged DI Blunt on Buster's whereabouts, then drove home.

Max and Donut had prepared a light meal for Marzia.

'Why do you always give me cherry juice with my meals?' asked Marzia, 'It tastes weird.'

We want to keep you nice and healthy,' said Max in jest.

'What time is the exchange?' enquired Marzia.

'It is tomorrow,' replied Max, 'Too many police are present for it to happen tonight.'

'You guys must be looking forward to a prison sentence,' mocked Marzia.

The two masked men bid Marzia goodnight, turned her bedroom light off, and locked the bedroom door.

Marshal drove to Bath, where he ventured through the city, and up to Bathwick Hill. It was a clear night with amazing views over the city. It was 11.30pm, when he telephoned the police station on Marzia's mobile phone.

'Good evening, this is Detective Constable Dolivo, how may I help you?'

'This is the Getaway Gang. The Marzia Bonanno exchange is off. Repeat, the exchange is off. We will give you a new location for another drop in the morning; the next drop will take place tomorrow night. There is too much police presence at Parkway station for it to go ahead.'

'But sir,' answered DC Dolivo, almost panicking, 'All the money is there, just as you asked, £500,000.'

'Take good care of our money until tomorrow night, and we will take good care of Marzia Bonanno,' instructed Marshal. 'Next time, no police; repeat, no police are to be anywhere near the drop off point.' Marshal hung up.

DC Dolivo telephoned DI Blunt with the news and the reason for the abandonment. The Inspector was livid; he swore. He called across to the two officers sitting in the unmarked police car. He told them of the cancelled pick up, and asked,

Crime is a Killer

'What chance of a road block back into Bristol? We could check vehicles for a voice changing device; if we find one, we will have caught a member of the Getaway Gang.'

DI Blunt walked over to the security vehicle with the news.

The Road Policing Unit collaborated with the Inspector's request, and set up a road block on the M32 motorway into Bristol. Marshal got lucky that night; feeling rather pleased with himself, he drove the less direct route back to the city, along the A4.

CHAPTER 11

The next morning, Buster and Yosef were on baby-sitting duty at the house. Buster had driven over to Woodlands Golf and Country Club, parking his car in what looked to be the only car space on the road. Aaron Loughty, in pursuit of Buster, had to find somewhere to park. In that time, Buster jogged up a nearby track and jumped into Yosef's parked car, giving Aaron Loughty the slip once again.

Buster was dehydrated from the night before; he thought he should have left the Megalodon bar well before 1am. Yosef was keen to talk to Marshal about his telephone call with Mattheo Freud. Marshal had announced he was planning to drive to Chippenham for his next telephone call to the police station.

DI Blunt, DS Welles and DC's Durden and Dolivo had gathered at the storyboard in the office. They were all feeling nervous, agitated about how events had developed the previous evening. The security vehicle, which still contained the half a million pounds, was safely locked away in a police pound in Bristol.

The name Feodor Bykov was added to the storyboard; he was the owner of the Megalodon bar. News had arrived from the Metropolitan police; Niles Easter had been tailed the previous evening to Shenanigans, the bar where he worked as a doorman. DI Blunt thought it best to put Niles Easter on the backburner; maybe finance one more tail that evening, so he could be eliminated from the enquiry.

DC Durden reported that investigation into a grey Bristol plate van hire from Bristol dealerships had proven negative.

Crime is a Killer

'I realise this will consume valuable resource,' admitted DI Blunt, 'But, we are going to have to widen our search to dealerships beyond Bristol. I will try and talk to the Governor about more resource.

DS Welles had started going through Stefan Bonanno's top ten hit list.

'We have tracked the Russian Caleb Tchaikovsky, number one on the list; he appears to fly into the UK almost once a month. He flies into Heathrow, but we have yet to establish where he travels to when in the country,' reported DS Welles. 'Number two, Volker Von der Leyan, has not travelled to the UK for three years; he resides in Vienna, Austria. Number three, Linwood McGinn, lives in Glasgow; we found photographs on the internet of his kneecapping. It looked bad; he ended up having his lower leg amputated. It's no wonder Stefan Bonanno had Linwood McGinn high up on his list.'

'Quite;' responded DI Blunt, 'Have we had chance to look at any other names on the list?'

'The last name on the list, Herman Freud, is apparently deceased. Suspected murder case; tampered vehicle leading to a fatal road accident,' reported DS Welles. 'Number seven on the list, Dillon Kelleher, is from Bristol. That's interesting don't you think?'

'Quite a coincidence,' answered DI Blunt, 'Better find out why he's on Stefan Bonanno's list.'

At that point DI Blunt called the team brief to a close. They all agreed to remain in the office that morning, expecting a telephone call from the Getaway Gang.

Later that morning, news came through from the Gloucestershire Constabulary, via the Metropolitan Police, that when interviewed, Niles Easter had given a false name and address on where he was on the night of the abduction. This puzzled DI Blunt; perhaps he shouldn't be excluded from their enquiries after all.

DI Blunt telephoned the owner of the Megalodon bar, Feodor Bykov.

'Hello, is that Mr Feodor Bykov, owner of the Megalodon bar in Bristol,' asked DI Blunt.

'Yes, this is he,' came the reply in broken English.

'Good morning sir, I am Detective Inspector Marcel Blunt of the Avon and Somerset Police in Bristol. I would like to ascertain confirmation that two of your dancers, a Chelsea Lewandowski and a Hannah Nowak, were working at the Megalodon bar on the evening of ...' the Inspector recited the date.

'I don't know; I will call you back,' Feodor Bykov hung up the telephone.

The Inspector wasn't very happy with the Russian's response; would he know what number to call him back on? The Inspector called Feodor Bykov once more; it was on answer phone, he left a message with the telephone number to call.

Connor Jackson, or rather Sean McBurney (the name on his false driving licence) telephoned the vehicle hire company in Bath, extending the van hire for a further five days. Marshal had given Connor a bank debit card number to extend the hire contract.

Crime is a Killer

Marshal drove along the M4 motorway, exiting at junction seventeen, Chippenham. He turned into a village called Kington Saint Michael, three miles north of the town, where he called the police station on Marzia's mobile phone.

'Good morning, Detective Constable Durden speaking, how may I help you?'

'Is Detective Inspector Blunt in the office? This is the Getaway Gang.'

'He is, just a moment sir.' DC Durden switched the call onto loudspeaker, and started waving frantically at all her colleagues.

This got everyone's attention, including Detective Chief Superintendent Dawes-Drake.

'Hello caller, Detective Inspector Blunt here; can I say we were very disappointed you never collected the half a million pounds that we had arranged for you yesterday evening.'

The robotic voice of Marshal replied, 'Not half as disappointed as we were Inspector. We told you no police to be present at the drop point. There was an unmarked police car in the station car park; there were undercover policemen in the church grounds. If there is a police presence on tonight's drop, Marzia Bonanno gets it!'

'Is Marzia well and unharmed?' questioned DI Blunt. 'Can we speak to her?'

'She is well, and no, you can't speak to her,' came the reply. 'Is the money safe?'

'The money is perfectly safe,' confirmed DI Blunt, 'It is locked up in a security vehicle, in a police pound. You say there is to be a drop tonight, where exactly?'

'Bristol airport,' came the reply, 'There is a microlight hangar in the airport complex, hangar B12; the money is to be left inside the hangar. The hangar must be unlocked so we can access the money. And no deception; no police are to be on the airfield, or anyone anywhere near the hangar.'

'But caller, we will have to clear this with the airport authorities; this is a most unconventional demand,' expressed DI Blunt.

'That's your problem,' came the reply, 'Remember, if we are double-crossed like last night; Marzia gets it.' Marshal ended the call.

Everyone in the police department looked stunned.

'Bristol airport; how absolutely bizarre,' commented DCS Dawes-Drake. 'Who runs the bloody airport these days? Marcel, you and Bryce better get your asses over there, pretty damn quick.'

DC Durden searched the internet and acquired the name of the airport's Chief Executive Officer and his contact details.

'I'll call him, ahead of your visit there Marcel,' proposed DCS Dawes-Drake. 'I'll talk to traffic too; we will have to intercept these bandits on the roads leading from the airport. What about these characters we have under surveillance?'

'Niles Easter and Joe Billings Junior; we have tails on them tonight Guv,' confirmed DI Blunt. 'Lissy, are you okay to tie up with the Advanced Security Officer and get the money transferred to the airport. We will be there to help where we can. Levi, can you pick up on Stefan Bonanno's top ten list?'

'Yes Boss,' replied DC Dolivo, 'I was checking on the Bristol character earlier, Dillon Kelleher, he's an ex-copper!'

Crime is a Killer

DI Blunt frowned in astonishment; that's a twist he thought.

At 10am, DI Blunt had a scheduled call with Stefan Bonanno. The objective was to update Mr Bonanno on the previous night's exchange.

Stefan Bonanno, accompanied by two guards, arrived at a small guard's office in HMP. They waited for the telephone to ring; Stefan Bonanno was seated. The phone rang, bang on ten.

'Hello, Stefan Bonanno.'

'Hello Mr Bonanno, Detective Inspector Blunt here.'

'Is Marzia there; can I speak with her?' asked her father.

'Sorry Mr Bonanno, she isn't here, the exchange never happened last night after all,' declared DI Blunt.

'Not there! Never happened! Why?' hollered Stefan Bonanno.

The Inspector had to think of a convincing answer, and fast. 'We had several vehicles on the roads leading from the station. What put the kidnappers off; they had observed an unmarked car in the station car park.'

'You bungling idiots. I knew you boys in blue would make a complete mess of this,' ranted Stefan Bonanno, 'Is Marzia safe? Where is my money?'

'Yes, we are told by the kidnappers that Marzia is safe and well,' replied DI Blunt. 'Your money is safe too, locked in a security vehicle in a police pound. There will be another exchange tonight, we will catch them this time,'

'You had better not cock it up again Inspector,' growled Stefan Bonanno. 'Where is the exchange tonight?' he asked.

'I'm afraid we are not in a position to divulge that information,' answered DI Blunt, 'You must trust us Mr Bonanno, we won't make the same mistake this time.'

'Trust you! I don't trust you any further than I can throw you,' came his exasperated reply. 'No harm must come to my daughter, and my money must remain in safe hands officer. Do I make myself clear?' he ranted.

'We read you loud and clear Mr Bonanno, please don't worry,' DI Blunt tried to placate the prisoner. 'Same time tomorrow Mr Bonanno? With better news, next time.'

The conversation concluded.

Marshal returned to the house and sat down with Yosef and Buster.

'I have informed the police, there is to be another attempt to exchange Marzia for the money tonight,' explained Marshal.

'When? Where? How?' questioned Yosef.

'In the early hours of the morning. Bristol airport. There is a microlight hangar there; I have instructed the police to leave the money in there,' replied Marshal.

Both Yosef and Buster looked flabbergasted.

'Bristol airport, microlight hangar, this sounds crazy Marshal,' declared Yosef.

'Don't worry, I have keys to the hangar, in case it is locked; I have my own microlight in there,' revealed Marshal, 'Along with a few antiques; motor cycles, bicycles, trailers.'

'How do you plan to get the money out of the hangar?' asked Yosef.

Crime is a Killer

'I have this amazing trailer hitched up to a motor bike; I plan to load the money onto the trailer and drive to the boundary fence of the airport, where Connor, Max and Donut will be waiting for me in the van. We transfer the money to the van and bring it here to the safe house.'

'But Marshal, surely the police will have multiple roadblocks and unmarked cars waiting for you along the routes from the airport,' stated Yosef.

'I shall have a decoy set up, on one particular road, you don't need to know the details,' answered Marshal.

'What do you need me to do?' asked Yosef.

'Yosef, I would like you to stay at the house,' instructed Marshal. 'Let's put a sheet up at the kitchen window, or something to cover it. We can count and share out the money in the kitchen. Buster, is Chelsea working at the Megalodon tonight?'

'She is actually; one of the girls has phoned in sick,' replied Buster.

'Good,' responded Marshal, 'You must go there again tonight, for an alibi. Make sure you are followed by that Mercedes. Tomorrow we will all come here to dish out the money. Tomorrow Buster, you must shake off the tail once again; if you are in the car, park half a mile away, as before. Bring Chelsea with you. Did you manage to get that little lock-up off your friend to store your share of the money?'

'Yes, we have the keys. Chelsea picked them up earlier,' replied Buster.

'Good. Connor, can take Chelsea and your share of the money over to the lock up, while you take your car and that Mercedes back to your flat,' suggested Marshal.

'What about Marzia?' asked Yosef.

'She will be fine,' declared Marshal, 'Once we have unloaded the money, we can drop her in the city, blindfolded. She should be wearing that crazy pink jumpsuit she was wearing when we captured her. We will burn all of her other clothes.'

'So, Buster and Chelsea will be at the bar; Connor, Max and Donut will be with the van, collect the money, empty the money here, then dump the girl. I shall stay here at the house; what about Niles?' asked Yosef.

'I suspect he is being tailed too, but he is working as a doorman tonight, so he has an alibi,' confirmed Marshal.

'Marshal, won't the police be able to trace the microlight to you personally,' questioned Yosef.

'I have that covered Yosef, the registered owner of my microlight is Sean McBurney,' said Marshal with a mocking expression.

Yosef wanted to tell Marshal about the new information on Stefan Bonanno, but after much deliberation he held back; Marshal must concentrate on the exchange that night, he thought. Yosef and Buster left the house in Yosef's car. Yosef dropped off Buster, so he could walk back to his own vehicle, he looked out for the black Mercedes; but he couldn't see it anywhere. Marshal left the house and drove into a city centre multi-storey car park to make a few telephone calls. First was to Niles, to update him on the drop arrangements.

'All being well Niles, we will be counting and sharing out the money tomorrow, in the safe house,' claimed Marshal. 'I will get you to jump on an early train in the morning, from Paddington to Bath. I can pick you up from Bath station.'

Crime is a Killer

'Why Bath? Why not Bristol?' asked Niles.

'It's too risky for you to come to Bristol by train Niles, in case you are recognised. Bath is a safer bet,' declared Marshal.

The next call was to Max, outlining the details of the night ahead.

'I had better bring the shotgun Marshal; we might have to shoot our way out of a corner,' suggested Max.

'Let's hope we don't have to use it,' was Marshal's reply.

Marshal's plan was for Connor, Max and Donut to all meet at the house, to drive the hired van over to the airport. Marshal had sent a photograph to Donut and Connor, with the location on where to collect the ransom money. Another evening, Max thought, that he would not be able to see Chelsea; never mind, this kidnapping ordeal was too exciting to miss.

Marshal's next call was to Connor, to go over the details.

'As all this will be happening throughout the night, how are you going to explain your whereabouts to your parents?' asked Marshal.

'I shall just tell them I am stopping over at my friend Rocky's house. Rocky will cover for me; I can tell Rocky I'm out joy-riding again,' explained Connor.

'Okay, see you tonight Connor. Drive carefully, don't draw any attention to the vehicle; it shouldn't be very busy in the early hours of the morning,' lectured Marshal. 'You can stay over at the safe house once we have dropped Marzia off if you like.'

Connor agreed that would be a good idea. Marshal's final call was to Donut, with a vision on how he would see the night ahead developing.

'Donut, can you get hold of a strong pair of steel bolt / wire cutters, and a portable steel saw?' asked Marshal. 'When it gets dark tonight, we will need to cut through a section of the perimeter fence to the airport. There is a section of High 'V' security fencing, that appears to be quite weak and vulnerable.'

'No problem,' answered Donut, 'I can get both the cutters and saw from where I work.'

The two men agreed to meet that evening, at the house.

DI Blunt and DS Welles met with the airport Chief Operating Officer, Montgomery Lavers. The COO had taken a telephone call earlier from DCS Dawes-Drake, so he was briefed well on the possible exchange.

Mr Lavers took the officers to a large conference room where they were served refreshment. Mr Lavers had gathered a significant number of participants to meet with the officers and understand the events that were about to unfold. Airport Security Manager, Airport Security Planning Officer, Airport Director, Airport Fire Chief, Airport Operations Manager, Airport Logistics Operations Manager, Head of Airport Administration, and finally the Chief Constable assigned to Bristol Airport. DI Blunt was suitably impressed. The Inspector briefed the group on what to expect; a security vehicle was about to arrive containing half a million pounds. The Inspector asked if they could visit the microlight hangar B12, and be there to receive the security vehicle. The Airport Security Manager explained to the two officers how the hangar was on the very outskirts of the airport complex; well away from commercial flight paths. The hangar would be generally locked, with winter fast approaching.

Crime is a Killer

'One final thing,' asked DI Blunt, 'Is it possible to obtain a list of the microlight owners? And I would like to stress once more; no personnel of any kind must be in close proximity to the hangar. We can't afford any mistakes that might put the hostage at risk, as unfortunately we did yesterday evening.'

The Head of Airport Administration volunteered to ascertain the information on microlight ownership. A few members of the group accompanied the two police officers to the hangar B12. Within the hour the security vehicle had arrived at the hangar, and the ransom money was unloaded. It was carefully stacked in the centre of the hangar.

'So that's what half a million quid looks like,' said the Airport Fire Chief.

It was a dark overcast night; Marshal and Donut arrived at the airport boundary fence near the hangar. They wore high visibility jackets, posing as workmen. They cut through the weakened fence with the cutters and saw, then carefully lodged the fence back together. Marshal was inside the airport complex. He handed Donut his high vis vest; he was now dressed completely in black, including a black balaclava. He walked just one hundred yards to the microlight hangar, and unlocked the side door to the hangar. From a distance, the police were focusing on the main hydraulic operated bi-fold hangar doors left ajar, not the side door. Marshal was inside; it was in complete darkness. He shone his mobile phone torch onto the pile of money sacks in the middle of the hangar and smiled.

Marshal opened up one of the money sacks carefully, with his black-gloved hands, and stared at the many used fifty and twenty-pound notes inside. Let's get you little beauties loaded onto my motorbike trailer he thought to himself. Marshal started to load the sacks onto the trailer.

Crime is a Killer

CHAPTER 12

Once all the money sacks were on the trailer, Marshal sat on his motor bike to draw breath. There were not that many sacks, but they were quite heavy. He secured the sacks with a tarpaulin sheet wrapped over them. It was time to make that all important phone call to Connor, who had parked the van on the A38, near the airport.

'We are good to go Connor,' declared Marshal, who hung up the phone straight away.

Connor started the engine, looked at Donut and Max and howled, 'This is it guys, it's pay day.'

They turned off and drove down the Downside Road, when Connor yelled, 'Oh my God! There is a police road block.'

'Keep driving Connor,' instructed Max, 'It looks like they are stopping traffic from the other direction,' as Max exercised his trigger finger on his sawed-off shotgun.

Donut gave Connor directions as they turned off past the local golf club. Connor was instructed to drive without lights for the final one hundred yards. Donut had sprayed a series of white crosses on the grass verge, approaching the cut-through boundary fence.

The night was still. Marshal waited at the side door of the hangar. He couldn't see them properly, but he heard the vehicle arrive in the still of night. He started up the motorbike; it seemed to purr as it ticked over. Marshal remembered that the trailer would fit through the side door of the hangar. Once outside, Marshal quickly relocked the hangar door. With no lights on the motorbike, Marshal drove the one hundred yards over to the boundary fence. The trailer rattled as it drove over the grass; it seemed to find every bump in the ground, thought Marshal. Donut opened out the fence, allowing Marshal to drive onto the track, behind the van. The four men quickly loaded the money sacks into the van.

DI Blunt, DS Welles and several airport security staff were trying to keep watch on the hangar from a distance away. They all believed they could hear a motorbike, and the rattle of the trailer, but they couldn't see anything. DI Blunt radioed the lead car on a route from the airport, to inform them that there was some form of movement near the microlight hangar; possible suspects on the move.

Marshal figured the Goblin Combe crossroads might have a road block. So, he sped off in the opposite direction, and along the Downside Road, with his motorbike and empty trailer, until he reached the police road block. When he was approached by the police officer, Marshal showed his Avon & Somerset Police badge; a replica he had made of his original badge. The officer waved him on.

On route to the road block, Marshal signalled a white van, in the entrance to a local golf club, by sounding his horn and flashing his lights. The driver was Chadd Aitken. Chadd was once known as a fixer in a drug cartel; surprisingly never convicted, that's how he knew Marshal. Chadd also despised Stefan Bonanno with a passion. The head of the cartel, Stefan, had double-crossed Chadd on several occasions.

Connor drove along the Cooks Bridle Path, turning into Downside Road, in the direction of the city centre; his heart was in his mouth with all that money onboard. Max and Donut were sat in the front cab with Connor; Max had his sawed-off shotgun with him; it was loaded. Connor's van slowly overtook Chadd's white van with the sound of the horn. Connor pulled up at the police road block; there were two cars queueing in front of Connor. Chadd's vehicle pulled up behind Connor's van. There was only one police car, three policemen, on foot. Suddenly there was a screeching of tyres. Chadd's van accelerated past the parked vehicles in the queue and raced through the road block. The policemen looked startled. Two of the policemen jumped in their car and gave chase to the white van. The remaining policeman waved the first car on. It was then, Connor decided to drive off, through the road block. The police officer looked to identify the vehicle registration. Connor had blanked over the vehicle number plate, on Marshal's instruction. Connor drove off into the centre of Bristol without being challenged.

'I have to say,' blurted Max, 'Marshal is a genius; I didn't think his decoy would work, but it has!'

The white van turned onto the A38 and headed toward the city centre. He could see the blue flashing lights of the police car in his rear mirror. Knowing that the police car would now have his van in their sights, he turned left off the main road onto Barrow Street. Further down the road, by the local pub, Chadd pulled over so the police officers could question him. Both officers approached the van; Chadd was asked to step out of the vehicle. He hoped the two thousand pounds that Marshal would pay him was going to be worth it. Chadd had no other excuse for jumping the road block, other than it was late, and all he wanted to do was get home. The police did question his route, through the historic village of Barrow Gurney; Chad explained it was his preferred route home, through the village and along the A370. He was issued with a ticket for dangerous driving, and driving without due care and attention.

Connor drove the van up onto the drive of the safe house. Yosef was there to open the garage door. Once the van was safely inside the garage, they transferred the money sacks into the kitchen. Marshal had parked his motorbike and trailer half a mile from the house.

'So that's half a million pounds,' said Yosef.

'We had better think about exchanging Marzia,' suggested Marshal. 'Did we manage to dress her in her pink jumpsuit she wore at the concert?'

'Yes,' claimed Max, 'We had to be a little persuasive though.' Max held his shotgun in the air to demonstrate.

Marshal shook his head, 'Where's the blindfold? Let's get this over with.'

Marshal, Max and Donut put on their masks and ventured up to Marzia's bedroom. Connor put on his balaclava and proceeded to the garage. Yosef stayed with the money. He was tense; nursing all that money was nerve-racking.

'C'mon little lady, it's time to meet daddy,' said Marshal.

'You are not going to get away with this. My father will have you all swimming with the sharks,' bawled Marzia.

Marshal blindfolded Marzia. Max led her down the stairs, into the garage and bundled her into the back of the van. Max and Donut climbed in the back with her; Marshal climbed into the cab with Connor. Yosef opened the garage door. Connor reversed the van out of the garage.

'Where are we going Marshal?' asked Connor.

'Bridewell police station; it's important Marzia is placed in safe hands,' responded Marshal.

Connor gave Marshal a vacant stare. 'That's crazy,' answered Connor.

Crime is a Killer

They pulled up near the police station; it was 2.45am. Marshal took the blindfold off Marzia.

'That's where you have to go little lady,' suggested Marshal, pointing at the police station. 'Please give my fondest regards to your father.'

Marshal shoved Marzia in the direction of the station and climbed back into the van. Marzia was determined this time to memorize the van's registration, except it was covered over. With her hands tied behind her back, she was pleased the front door of the station opened inwardly. Marzia approached the front desk.

'Good evening,' said the Night Officer, 'Are you okay?' he asked.'

'I am Marzia Bonanno,' she replied, with tear-filled glazed eyes, 'I was kidnapped, and held hostage in a bedroom in a house here in Bristol.'

'Oh, my goodness,' came the reply. The Constable picked up the telephone to call the Detective Inspector on duty that evening.

DI Blunt was still at the airport; he was keen to talk to the traffic police on the Downside Road, to establish what had happened. His mobile phone rang. It was the front desk at Bridewell station, with the news that Marzia Bonanno had been delivered to the station. DI Blunt asked DS Welles to ascertain statements with the traffic police, while he returned to Bridewell station.

Marzia was sat in the DI's office when he arrived. He introduced himself; he thought Marzia looked exhausted and haggard.

'Do you have any idea Marzia, where the kidnappers held you?' asked the Inspector.

'It was definitely in Bristol,' answered Marzia. 'I could see a few high-rise buildings, church spire, and a tall yellow crane; it was a short ride in the back of a van from the Liberty Club.'

'Would you recognise it again Marzia?' asked the Inspector.

'Yes, I'm sure I could; I was imprisoned long enough with just one view through a bedroom window,' came her reply.

'Did you get a chance to see any of the kidnappers? Any descriptions, voice recognitions? Any idea how many there were?' asked the Inspector.

I counted seven, maybe eight,' replied Marzia. 'One was a girl; she wore a mask, she had long blonde hair. She brought me different changes of clothes and underwear, all newly purchased.'

DI Blunt scribed down; Chelsea Lewandowski?

'The seven versus eight; there was one guy who I only heard on the first night. He had a deep voice, with an African, almost American twang,' reported Marzia.

DI Blunt scribed again; Niles Easter?

'There was one guy with an eastern European accent, Romanian, Albanian maybe. He wore a president's mask. He was very scruffy. On several days he seemed to be covered in dust; it was as if he worked on a building site. He didn't say very much; I felt he was afraid I would recognise his accent,' advised Marzia.

DI Blunt made a note of the accent and the man's attire.

'There was one really scary guy,' exclaimed Marzia, 'He had a sawed-off shotgun; he even let off the gun and shot the bathroom door when I was inside. He also wore a president's mask. He was dressed in commando gear most of the time; camouflage jacket, almost military appearance. He scared me, often threatened me with his shotgun. He was in the back of the van when they kidnapped me, when they dropped me here at the station, and when they drove somewhere for an hour or more to speak to you guys.'

'Ah yes, that was Swindon,' claimed the Inspector, 'We were able to trace your mobile phone. The kidnappers used your mobile phone to call the station each time, to discuss the ransom and pick-up points.'

'You can trace my phone? Where is it now?' asked Marzia.

'Right now, we don't know,' replied the Inspector. 'They have a way of disconnecting the signal somehow.' The Inspector wrote down some notes on the gunman.

'There was a guy, who seemed to be in charge. He was tall, six-foot, well spoken, quite authoritative, smart casual dresser; he too wore a mask, of our Prime Minister,' explained Marzia.

'I am very interested in hearing more about this character,' responded the Inspector.

'There was a more elderly guy, short, frail, quietly spoken, wore a monster's mask. He was dressed like a business man; jacket, trousers, shirt and tie,' enlightened Marzia.

'There was one cheeky guy, strong local accent, bragged about stealing my father's money,' claimed Marzia. 'He wore a superheroes mask, jeans, t-shirt. I took an instant dislike to him.'

'That's seven Marzia, is there an eighth?' asked the Inspector.

'Yes, a younger guy; he wore a black balaclava, local accent, piercing light blue eyes, snappy dresser,' suggested Marzia. 'I would like to take a shower somewhere, and change my clothes, if possible, I feel grubby Inspector.'

'There is a facility here at the station where you can shower; we will try and find you some new clothes to wear. We will need to forensically check your clothing for prints, DNA etc. Before you leave us, we would need to take your prints and DNA,' explained the Inspector. 'Can you still be here at ten, this morning? I have a scheduled telephone call with your father. He would love to hear from you and know you are safe. You must be exhausted?'

'Quite the opposite Inspector,' said Marzia, 'I'm sure they were drugging me; I slept continuously whilst in that house. I would love to speak to my father Inspector, but what about his money? Did he really put up half a million pounds?'

'Yes, he did,' clarified the Inspector. 'Don't worry, we will recover the money.'

'They have the money!' shrieked Marzia, 'Oh my God, my father is going to be so mad.'

Buster and Chelsea walked to the bus stop. Buster glanced at the black Mercedes, but he had a plan. They took a ride on the bus into the city centre. They jumped off the bus outside a departmental store, and went inside. Aaron Loughty pulled up behind the bus and thought, bugger, they have given me the slip again. Buster and Chelsea came out of a different exit to flag down a taxi to go to the house. When they arrived, everyone was there; even Niles, who had been picked up by Marshal earlier, from Bath railway station. Everyone took great pleasure in counting the money into quantities of sixty thousand pounds.

Marzia reappeared in some temporary clothing; she still looked hot, thought DI Blunt. The Inspector had been working with his team that morning, updating the information that Marzia Bonanno had provided.

It was time to call Stefan Bonanno. The same arrangement as the previous day had been set up.

'Hello, Stefan Bonanno.'

'Good morning Mr Bonanno, Detective Inspector Blunt here with.'

Marzia took the phone, 'Daddy, it's Marzia,'

'Oh! Thank God,' murmured Stefan Bonanno. He broke down and wept for a few seconds. 'You are safe. Did they harm you? I will kill them if they harmed you.'

'No Daddy, they didn't harm me, just threatened me a few times,' claimed Marzia. 'Thank you, for putting up so much money for my release; I love you Daddy.'

Stefan Bonanno reacted, 'Money, yes the money. Is it safe? The police have it safe, don't they?'

DI Blunt intervened, 'They took the money Mr Bonanno. We were unable to go to the drop point, the visibility was poor, they jumped a road block. But don't worry Mr Bonanno, we will recover the money.'

'You bungling idiots, I will kill them, I will kill you,' shouted Stefan Bonanno. At that point DI Blunt hung up the telephone.

'I told you my father would be mad,' implied Marzia.

DI Blunt stopped by DCS Dawes-Drake's office to update him on Marzia's information received so far, and Stefan Bonanno's reaction to the Getaway Gang being in possession of the half a million pounds.

'I decided to cut Stefan Bonanno off Guv, he started to get very aggressive and personal,' claimed DI Blunt.

'Well at least he will have a few hours to calm down and accept the facts, before you meet him face to face Marcel,' said DCS Dawes-Drake.

DI Blunt looked bemused.

DCS Dawes-Drake continued, 'I have taken a call from the Hampshire Constabulary; there was a fatal car accident in Hayling Island. There is a suspected murder case of a Herman Freud. The police there are in possession of a threatening email from Stefan Bonanno, demanding £195,000. Hampshire have assigned a DI Gail Fishar to interview Stefan Bonanno later today in HMP. I have volunteered you Marcel, to accompany her.'

'Thanks Guv, good job I can be a bit thick-skinned with the abuse I am likely to receive off of Stefan Bonanno,' replied DI Blunt.

'There's one more thing Marcel,' continued DCS Dawes-Drake, 'We couldn't have put an end time on Niles Easter's tail. The private detective followed Niles across London on the tube this morning; he took the train from Paddington to Bristol Temple Meads.'

'Niles Easter is in Bristol!' snapped DI Blunt. 'I'll get Levi to check out CCTV footage at Temple Meads train station. Let's hope he was met by a partner in crime at the station, and we get them both on CCTV.'

'It makes sense, if he did arrive back in Bristol this morning. I expect the Getaway Gang are apportioning Stefan Bonanno's half a million pounds as we speak,' implied DCS Dawes-Drake.

DI Blunt decided it was time to call Feodor Bykov once more.

'Hello, this is Feodor Bykov.'

'Detective Inspector Blunt here Mr Bykov; did you get a chance to check on Chelsea and Hannah from your rota?'

'Yes, I pay Hannah, I not pay Chelsea,' came his reply.

'Which implies that Chelsea wasn't working that evening?' questioned DI Blunt.

'She may have worked. If she did, I did not pay her,' answered the Russian.

DI Blunt put the telephone down and thought it was time to make some arrests; Joe Billings Junior, Chelsea Lewandowski and Niles Easter for starters.

Marzia Bonanno sat down with DC Durden and went through some outfit identification for what the Getaway Gang members were wearing during her abduction. DS Welles was waiting to drive Marzia around Bristol, to see if she could recognise any landmarks from where she was held as a hostage. DC Durden gave Marzia the contact number for Adam her ex-bodyguard. She telephoned Adam from the station. He was overcome and tearful, to hear her voice. He explained to her that her father had terminated his employment; this saddened Marzia. Adam had her suitcase from touring in his possession. He agreed to collect her from Bridewell police station at 2pm.

By the late lunchtime, the half a million pounds had been counted, verified and allotted into piles of £60,000.

'What happens to the other £20,000 Marshal,' asked Buster.

'There is likely to be a further share after expenses,' said Marshal. 'I will pay the decoy £2,000, but I consider that was money well spent; it worked prodigiously. I shall pay Yosef for the six months house rental. There is the van hire, furniture upstairs which we hired, purchase of mobile phones, plus some other expenses. I will send you all a detailed breakdown of expenses later,' responded Marshal.

Yosef opened up with all the gang listening in, on how his financial controller was brutally murdered and how the police are investigating a demand of £195,000 from Stefan Bonanno. This news got everyone's full attention.

'That's very interesting,' said Marshal, 'We may not be finished yet with Mr Stefan Bonanno.'

There was a chuckle, a buzz of excitement around the room. Marshal collected everyone's mobile phones to have them destroyed. He promised to post new phones to everyone. He urged everyone not to spend the cash in Bristol; the further afield the better. He explained that despite acquiring the abduction money sprightly, the bank should have recorded at least some of the serial numbers of the bank notes. He also explained that Marzia would be asked by the police to provide descriptions of everyone. Despite us all wearing gloves and masks all the time, she would be able to identify what everyone was wearing. He urged them all to either destroy the clothes, or make sure they weren't worn again for a very long time.

Crime is a Killer

There was a silence around the room; the gang members were all comprehending what Marshal had just said to them.

'When is our next job?' asked Buster.

'Let's get over this one first Buster,' replied Marshal, 'It was certainly an adrenaline high operation.'

'Only in the city centre I have seen a jeweller shop having restoration work,' explained Buster. 'It is surrounded by scaffolding; there is a quiet alleyway up the side of the building. No CCTV off the main street that I can see. There is what looks like a boiler room on the roof that could be broken into. Some of you might know it; Gold Schmist and Steinmann, in Broadmead.'

'I know it well Buster,' replied Marshal, 'I have bought jewellery for my ex-girlfriend Valesca from there a few times. When I was on the patch, it was burgled once before. The electrical circuit breakers and alarm controls were all situated on the first floor. Should you enter from the roof, you could possibly disconnect all of the alarms. Interesting Buster, I will take a look, and check it out. Hypothetically everyone, before we all go our separate ways, who would be in, or prefer out, should this heist on the jewellers go ahead?'

Niles declined as it was Bristol. Yosef had too many friends and acquaintances in and around Broadmead, so he too declined. Chelsea declined as she is determined to start a new life with hers, and Buster's £60,000. Max looked at her scornfully.

'That's a five-way split then,' announced Marshal. 'Thank you everyone, for your dedication and commitment in robbing Stefan Bonanno of his half a million quid. Now, let's get this cash out of here.'

Crime is a Killer

CHAPTER 13

Marshal attempted to organise the distribution of the ransom money.

'Connor, if we load Buster and Chelsea's money sacks into the van, you could take them to their lock-up, unload the money, and then drop them off at their flat,' suggested Marshal. 'Be aware of that black Mercedes though; maybe drop them off round the corner.'

Buster and Chelsea, with Connor's help, started moving their share of the money.

'Yosef, while Connor is doing that, you could move your car into the garage; we can start loading your share of the ransom,' proposed Marshal. 'You do have somewhere to hide the money Yosef, don't you?' asked Marshal.

'In the grounds of our property, we have a lockable, secluded summer house. We will keep it in there, well away from the main house,' answered Yosef.

'Niles, later on Connor and I can take you back to London in the van, with your share of the money. Do you have plans on where to keep it safe?' asked Marshal.

'Yes Marshal, we plan to keep it at Makena's father's house. He has a garage which he seldom enters these days. He is elderly and not so mobile,' replied Niles.

'Donut, what are your plans?' asked Marshal.

Donut explained, 'When I first moved to Avonmouth, I shared a caravan with Alexandru and Patrin, that was very cramped. So, we have a second caravan now, where Patrin stays. He wants to return to Romania, so the plan is, he will take £10,000 to Romania with him. He may lose a little when he exchanges the pounds sterling at Bucharest, but that is okay. That should be enough money for a fresh start back in Transylvania for him. Alexandru and I will share the remaining £50,000. It will be locked away in Patrin's caravan.'

'Sounds a plan,' said Marshal. 'What's your plans Max?'

'I have a boarded loft at home,' he replied, 'It will have to go in there temporarily. I might acquire a lock up outside of Bristol, where I can store and trade weaponry and ammunition. I could move some of the money there, if it materialises.'

'Be careful Max, that's all I can say on that scheme,' responded Marshal.

Connor came back in from the garage, 'All loaded. Buster and Chelsea are ready to rock and roll.'

'Where are you going to keep your money Connor?' asked Marshal.

'I might have to keep it here locked in the van for a few days,' he replied, 'My plan is to store it in my mate Rocky's house, in his loft. We need his folks to be out of the house for a while, in order to move the money.'

'Mm, let me know if that becomes a problem,' said Marshal. 'I have a concealed basement at my house in Clifton. Worst case scenario, we could hide it in there for a while. Is your friend Rocky getting a cut?' he asked.

'I might have to throw him some notes from time to time,' answered Connor.

'Try and discourage him from spending any of it in Bristol,' advised Marshal.

Crime is a Killer

Connor, Buster and Chelsea set off with their money. Yosef drove his Bentley from two streets away, into the garage. He was watched carefully by a very nosy neighbour; a Mrs Lewisham.

DI Blunt was on route to HMP to meet DI Fishar and Stefan Bonanno, when he took a call from DS Welles.

'Boss, I have just driven Marzia around several districts of Bristol. We set off from the Liberty Club. She recognised a couple of high-rise buildings and a church in Lawrence Hill. So, where she was held captive, we can narrow the search down to Lawrence Hill, Ashley, Central, Easton, Windmill Hill, possibly Brislington West,' reported DI Welles.

'That's great Bryce,' replied DI Blunt, 'Let's get those districts up onto the storyboard, get the team thinking about possibilities. Why don't you grab either Levi or Lissy, to drive around a few of those districts for a while; see if you can spot anything out of the ordinary. Maybe, have a word with the Superintendent; it might be worth putting out a statement on the local news channels this evening. Also, just check with the Super, I am looking to bring in for questioning Joe Billings Junior, Chelsea Lewandowski and Niles Easter. It would be great if we could rush through search warrants for their properties; we might find some money belonging to Stefan Bonanno.'

'Will do Boss,' came the answer.

DS Parkin and DC Jha of the Metropolitan Police paid a second visit to the home of Niles Easter. Niles never invited the officers into his home, their questioning took place at the front door. DS Parkin explained that the address Niles had given him for his stay in Gloucester was a false address.

Niles claimed there must be some kind of mistake. He produced a piece of paper from his wallet, with that address written on it. DS Parkin continued that line of questioning, claiming that Niles had caught a train from Paddington to Bristol. He was asked, what was his business in Bristol? Niles made a point of telling the officer that he hadn't gone to Bristol; he disembarked the train at Bath. He claimed he could be seen on CCTV leaving Bath railway station at approximately 8.55am. The two officers made a note of the time quoted by Niles, thanked him and left. Niles felt a little apprehensive that he was followed to Paddington that morning, and to which train he had caught.

Buster and Marshal had exchanged mobile telephone numbers, in case the jeweller's heist was a possibility.

'Do you have any contacts Marshal, that you can offload jewellery to?' asked Buster.

'Yes, I have a man in Birmingham, an ex-copper, that I believe can help,' replied Marshal.

'I have some jewellery that I don't know how to shift, from a recent house robbery,' claimed Buster, 'Can I show it to you sometime?'

'Why not,' came the answer, 'Wait until that Mercedes tail cools off. Make sure it isn't parked near your flat, then you can bring the jewellery over to my place.'

DCS Dawes Drake made contact with Assistant Chief Constable Grantham Foy in the Police Press Office. He updated the ACC with the facts on Marzia Bonanno's release from captivity. ACC Foy promised to update the local television and radio stations, create a statement for social media and update the NPCC, National Police Chiefs Council. The two officers agreed to use the photographs of Marzia and Stefan Bonanno, that had been shown on previous news bulletins.

Back at the house, operations were going to plan. Yosef and Marshal had removed their shares of the ransom. Connor had returned to load Donut's, Max's, and his own quota onto the van. Periodically, Mrs Lewisham would watch what was going on from her front room window.

DI Blunt arrived at HMP and met up with DI Gail Fishar in the visitors' cafeteria. They exchanged facts on Herman Freud's accident and Marzia Bonanno's abduction, and touched on the disappearance of Stefan Bonanno's half a million pounds. DI Fishar thought this might turn out to be the most interesting interview, ever.

Stefan Bonanno was sat in a small interview room, with two guards in attendance. DI Fishar entered the room first and introduced herself. Then DI Blunt entered the room. Stefan Bonanno quickly stood up, glaring at the Inspector. The guards moved toward Stefan Bonanno in order to restrain him.

'You have a nerve showing your face in here Inspector,' bellowed Stefan Bonanno. His fists were clenched.

'Mr Bonanno, please don't worry, we will recover your money. We are about to arrest three people who we believe may have been involved with the abduction of your daughter. Plus, Marzia is well and helping us with our enquiries,' claimed DI Blunt.

'Which three people?' asked Stefan Bonanno, 'Are they on my list?'

'No, they are not on your list, and we are not in a position to divulge their identities at this stage,' answered DI Blunt, with a smug look on his face.

Stefan Bonanno had a more contemptuous look on his face, as he sat back down in his chair.

'I am here on this occasion for continuity, Mr Bonanno,' expressed DI Blunt, 'My colleague, DI Fishar, would like to ask you a few questions about a certain gentleman who is on your list.'

Stefan Bonanno's eyes locked onto DI Fishar; he wore a frown, not knowing what to expect.

'Thank you, Marcel,' said DI Fishar. 'Mr Bonanno, how well did you know Herman Freud?'

Stefan Bonanno looked startled. 'Not that well. He was a financial director, who dabbled in stocks and shares. I bought and sold shares from his organisation occasionally. Why,' he asked.

DI Blunt interrupted, 'Why was Herman Freud tenth on your list of gents most likely to have kidnapped your daughter?'

'He owes me money for the sale of shares,' came the answer.

'How much money?' questioned DI Fishar.

'I can't remember,' claimed Stefan Bonanno.

'Was it £195,000?' she asked.

Stefan Bonanno looked stunned. He wanted to know how the Detective knew the exact value.

Crime is a Killer

'Possibly, I really can't remember,' answered Stefan incoherently.

'Mr Bonanno, Herman's son Mattheo has kindly forwarded on to my police department, a demanding email from yourself. In this email the demands are clear; it was for the sale of shares worth £195,000,' confirmed DI Fishar.

'Someone must have sent that email on my behalf. I can't remember sending a demanding email, that's not like me to do that,' snapped Stefan Bonanno.

The two detectives looked at each other in amazement.

'That is a lot of money to lose. I'm so sorry for you Mr Bonanno,' said DI Fishar.

'Lose. What do you mean, lose?' questioned Stefan Bonanno.

'Well now Herman Freud isn't alive anymore, it is likely to be a matter for the courts to arbitrate,' expressed DI Fishar.

'Freud is dead? How?' roared Stefan Bonanno.

'He was murdered; his car was tampered with,' came the Detective's reply.

'Murdered,' exclaimed the prisoner. There was a deathly silence. 'Oh, I see, you think I may have had something to do with it. Well, I wasn't keen on the man, I'm not sure I trusted him even, but I had no reason to kill him. I'm not saying anything else without my solicitor present.'

'Not one of your better days Mr Bonanno; £500,000 from the kidnapping and now this news,' taunted DI Fishar.

The prisoner glared at the Inspector but said nothing.

'One more thing Mr Bonanno, totally changing the subject,' interrupted DI Blunt, 'Dillon Kelleher was seventh on your list. I understand he is an ex-policeman. Why is he on the list; did he arrest you?'

'No,' replied Stefan Bonanno, 'He used to feed me information on drug movements, timescales. I grassed on him. He got discharged from the force and banged up for it. I thought he might want to get even, one day.'

That's interesting, thought DI Blunt.

The two officers closed the discussion with DI Fishar asking Stefan Bonanno to have a long hard think about who could have possibly sent the demanding email on his behalf, to Herman Freud.

Marshal drove into the city centre and parked in St James Barton multi-storey car park, near Broadmead. He stood for quite a while, studying the restoration work on the Gold Schmist and Steinmann jewellers. Marshal ventured up the alleyway to the side of the shop; there were some good blind spots, and Buster was right; there was no CCTV visible. There was also a side door, with just enough clearance under the erected scaffolding. Perfect escape route, thought Marshal. He continued down the alleyway into an adjoining road; a good location for Connor to park a getaway vehicle, he thought. On his return, he studied what Buster called the boiler room on the roof of the building. It was of brick construction, with a wooden painted, shabby door. Might be an idea to ask Donut to take a look at that, thought Marshal. He ventured into the shop; there was only one other customer in there. The only assistant was keen to ask Marshal if he thought all the scaffolding surrounding the shop was enough to put customers off? Marshal shook his head. He showed particular interest in a watch display on the back wall of the shop. From this point Marshal could clearly see behind the counter. He was curious to see if there was a panic button; he couldn't see one. He bid the shop assistant good day, and left for home, feeling quite satisfied with his scouting mission.

When Marshal arrived home, Buster's car was parked on his double-drive. Buster had two cardboard boxes, with jewellery from an earlier robbery.

'Bring them in Buster, we can keep them in my basement for now,' announced Marshal. Marshal opened a cupboard door under a staircase; it was empty inside. On the far wall of the cupboard was a door lock; Marshal unlocked it to enter a concealed basement. He switched on a light, down eight stone steps, to a large basement with many valuables, including a suit of armour.

'Wow,' claimed Buster, 'This is absolutely amazing Marshal. You would never know this was here.'

The basement had no windows; only one of the brick walls was plastered. On that wall were a few shelves with valuables on them. Buster noticed in opposite corners of the basement, two stacks of money sacks; one labelled Marshal, and one labelled Connor.

'So, Connor brought his money here?' asked Buster.

'Yes,' replied Marshal, 'Connor was planning to hide his share of the money in his friend's loft. This Rocky character, that Connor speaks so highly of, wanted half of the money! Connor wanted to keep his share in the van, at the house, but we really need to return the vehicle to the hire company. I would expect the police to be searching for it.'

Buster fetched the second box of jewellery from his car and placed it in Marshal's basement. He also brought over the wig that Chelsea had worn on the night of the abduction, for Marshal to destroy.

'This jewellery may as well stay here for now Buster,' suggested Marshal, 'We can take it to Birmingham to have it valued with the next pickings.'

'Next pickings, what next pickings?' asked Buster.

'Gold Schmist and Steinmann of course,' claimed Marshal. 'I'm going to ask Donut next, what he thinks of breaking into the jewellers from that building on the roof.'

'We're going to rob the jewellers! Ah, Marshal, you're the man,' implied Buster, as he embraced the ex-policeman with an excitable bear hug.

Crime is a Killer

Marshal gave Buster his new mobile telephone, only to be used for the jewellery shop heist. Marshal had packaged up ready for posting, new mobile phones for Max, Donut and Connor. Buster put his new phone in the glove box of his car, and drove back to his flat.

Marshal had agreed to meet Connor and Niles at the house, load up Niles' quota of ransom and drive him back to London.

Buster arrived back at the flat only to see two police cars parked up close by. That unnerved Buster. Chelsea was at home; she greeted him with a warm embrace.

'There are two police cars in the street; I wonder what they are doing?' said Buster.

At that moment came several loud bangs on their front door. Buster and Chelsea froze for a moment, before Buster answered the door. Four police officers stood on their balcony.

Buster recognised DI Blunt. The Inspector asked, 'Joe Billings Junior, is Chelsea at home? May we speak with you both together?'

'Yes of course,' replied Buster, rather sheepishly. 'Chelsea,' he called. Chelsea came to the front door.

'Joe Billings Junior and Chelsea Lewandowski, we would like you both to accompany us down to the police station,' announced DI Blunt. 'We **arrest** you both; for false imprisonment involving unlawful and intentional, or reckless detention of Marzia Bonanno against her will. In addition, the dishonest taking of property belonging to

Stefan Bonanno, with the intention of permanently depriving him of that property. You **do** not have to say anything, but it may harm your defence if you **do** not mention when questioned, something which you later rely on **in** court. Anything you do say, may be given in evidence.'

The blood drained out of Chelsea's face; she looked horrified. Buster felt his bottom lip quivering with nerves. He noticed DC Dolivo holding up a pair of handcuffs.

'There is no need for those,' stammered Buster, 'We will come quietly.'

Despite Buster's offer, DC Dolivo cuffed himself to Buster, and DC Durden cuffed herself to Chelsea.

One hour later, Marshal arrived at the house. Connor and Niles had just finished loading Niles' ransom money into the van. Connor reversed the van onto the street; Niles was sitting in the cab with Connor. Marshal closed and locked the garage door when Mrs Lewisham appeared.

'Hello, I'm Mrs Lewisham. You are new here, aren't you?' she said.

Marshal approached her and showed her his replica police badge.

'Yes, I'm Detective Inspector Blunt,' answered Marshal, giving her a false name; a name used by Buster when questioned recently. 'I am on a temporary assignment here for Avon and Somerset Police, so I have rented this property for a few months.'

'That's comforting, to know we have a police officer as a neighbour,' replied Mrs Lewisham.

Crime is a Killer

'If you will excuse me, Mrs Lewisham, duty calls.' Marshal jumped in the van and told Connor to drive on. 'Nosy old bitch,' he whispered to Niles and Connor.

Mrs Lewisham watched the van drive off, and made a mental note of the vehicle registration. Connor had removed the number plate shielding, after dropping Marzia Bonanno off at the police station.

One thing that Buster and Chelsea hadn't bargained for was a night in a police cell. DI Blunt informed them that they would both be interviewed at 10am the next morning. They would both be accompanied by a solicitor, offered at no cost, compliments of Avon and Somerset Police. Buster was curious of this arrangement. How could he challenge this disposition for corruption, should he need to? They were asked to hand over their personal belongings. Buster's heart almost missed a beat when he handed over his original mobile phone; he had Marshal's number amongst his contacts. Buster held back his house and car keys, in his inside jacket pocket. Chelsea handed over her keys. DI Blunt announced that they had warrants to search their flat. He produced the document, which they read carefully. The couple looked at each other with fear in their eyes.

Conner, Niles and Marshal arrived at Makena's father's home in north London. Makena was there, waiting for Niles to arrive. The three men unloaded Niles' quota into the garage, whilst Makena sat with her father to capture his undivided attention. The task was challenging; the garage was very busy with an old car, lawn mower, tools and garden sundries, and now money sacks.

Donut left it until it was dark to pay a visit to the jewellers, Gold Schmist and Steinmann. He climbed the scaffolding ladder with ease and was soon on the building's roof terrace. He inspected the door lock with his flashlight; it had a key operated lock. Donut had acquired a set of primary keys from his workplace; a set of keys designed to open multiple locks. The key with the red mark on it opened the door. Donut smiled, and relocked the door. Donut quietly climbed down the ladder. He was keen to provide some positive feedback to Marshal.

10am next morning, DS Welles started the interview, having already quoted the date.

'It is 10am. I am Detective Sergeant Bryce Welles and I am accompanied by Detective Constable Lissy Durden. In the room is Chelsea Lewandowski, and representing Chelsea is solicitor, Gloria Steadman.'

In an adjacent interview room, DI Blunt turned on the recorder to announce.

'It is 10.05 am. I am Detective Inspector Marcel Blunt, accompanied by Detective Constable Levi Dolivo. In the room is Joe Billings Junior. Joe is represented by solicitor, Dominic Ludlow.'

The first question to Chelsea from DS Welles was where she was on the night of the Goddess of Rock concert. Was she at the Liberty Club?

'I was working at the Megalodon bar that night. I have already told the Inspector this. Another dancer, Hannah, was also questioned by the Inspector, and she confirmed we were both at the bar that night,' answered Chelsea.

'We have that statement on record Miss Lewandowski,' replied DS Welles. 'However, we made contact with the bar's owner, a Mr Feodor Bykov. He confirmed to us that you were not on the rota that evening, and that you were not paid for that evening; although your colleague Hannah was paid.'

'He doesn't know what goes on in the Bristol bar,' responded Chelsea. 'He lives in London; we hardly ever see him.'

'Surely Miss Lewandowski, you would miss the money, not being paid for working that evening?' questioned DS Welles. 'Wouldn't you have challenged Mr Bykov for not paying you?'

'You have no idea how it all works,' replied Chelsea. 'The wage for the evening is a minimum wage. The owner pays us once a month. We make far more money putting on a show, or with private dancing. In an eight-hour shift, I can earn six-times my wage, easily. We are supposed to declare what we take and give twenty-five percent back to the owner. That doesn't happen, which demonstrates the owner's inability to control what he pays his dancers.'

'Thank you, Miss Lewandowski. How can you explain however, not being on the rota?' questioned DS Welles.

'We often fill in for girls not turning up for work,' replied Chelsea. 'Last night is a good example. I should have been working, but I had to spend the night in your rotten police cell.'

'Can anyone else witness you were working the night of the concert; another dancer, or customer?' questioned DS Welles.

'My boyfriend Buster was there for part of the evening,' came her reply.

DS Welles tried an alternative attack, 'Miss Lewandowski, do you happen to own a long-haired black wig?'

'No, I don't,' lied Chelsea.

DS Welles went on to inform Chelsea that she wouldn't be allowed home that evening, as their flat was still being searched by a police forensic team.

Chelsea's mouth went dry; she reached for a glass of water. She hoped Buster had disposed of the wig as he had promised. Suddenly Chelsea was very scared.

DS Welles asked Chelsea if she knew Marzia Bonanno, or her father Stefan, or had she ever heard of her band Goddess of Rock. Chelsea denied knowing Marzia, Stefan or the band, other than the news bulletins on television.

Toward the end of the interview Chelsea asked her solicitor how long the police could detain her.

'The police can only hold you for up to 24 hours; after that they can apply for an extension to 36 or 96 hours, but they would have to charge you, and I don't consider that they have the necessary evidence,' claimed Chelsea's assigned solicitor Gloria Steadman.

In another interview room, Buster was interrogated by DI Blunt in a similar vein to Chelsea's interview. Where was he on the night of Marzia Bonanno's abduction? He was quite adamant with his reply, at the Megalodon bar. Did he know Marzia or Stefan Bonanno? His answer was quite clear, no, other than the recent news on television. Did he possess a long black wig? No, he did not. Did Buster or Chelsea have any friends or family living in the Lawrence Hill district? This line of questioning made Buster feel somewhat uneasy; his answer was no.

DI Blunt was called out of room, so he temporarily terminated the interview. A Second Line IT Support Analyst appeared with both Chelsea's and Buster's mobile phones. Matches on Chelsea's contacts had proven negative. There was one match on Buster's phone; a phone registered to Dillon Kelleher, with a contact name of Marshal. DI Blunt re-entered the room, and reconvened the interrogation.

'Mr Billings, we have your mobile phone here. My IT department have run a contacts match; there is one number that is of interest to us, registered to a Dillon Kelleher,' declared DI Blunt.

At first the name didn't register with Buster; he shook his head and frowned.

'You have the contact number as Marshal,' stated DI Blunt, 'How do you know this Marshal?'

'Ah, Marshal,' responded Buster, 'We were in prison at the same time; that is what everyone called him in prison.'

'Did you know this Marshal character very well?' asked DI Blunt, 'I see you made a recent phone call to his mobile telephone.'

'Not that well,' indicated Buster, 'I just wanted to know if he had landed any work since leaving prison. I haven't had much luck finding work.'

'For someone that you don't know very well Mr Billings, your telephone call had a duration of twenty-two minutes,' divulged DI Blunt.

'Just catching up, general condition of the job market, what it's like outside HMP,' avowed Buster.

'In prison, did Mr Kelleher ever mention Stefan Bonanno?' questioned DI Blunt.

'I don't remember,' professed Buster, 'Why do you ask?'

'Stefan Bonanno produced a list of the most likely people to abduct his daughter Marzia. Dillon Kelleher was on the list. Stefan Bonanno leaked information that put the ex-detective in prison. So, would you say, he might have mentioned his name, in all those hours of solitude?' enquired DI Blunt.

'Hey, if he did, I don't recall, I am useless with names,' alleged Buster.

Toward the close of the interview, DI Blunt announced that a forensic team were still examining his and Chelsea's flat. They would both have to spend another evening under arrest. This angered Buster; his acting solicitor Dominic Ludlow had to explain the conditions of an arrest, and the potential timescales involved.

'Wait a minute,' yelled Buster, 'How did your forensic team gain access to the flat?'

DI Blunt smiled, 'Miss Lewandowski gave us her keys. They will be returned safely.'

DI Blunt terminated the interview and left the room. He turned to DC Dolivo and said, 'I think it is time to pay a visit to Dillon Kelleher.'

The next morning, Marshal, Connor and Max arrived at the house. Buster should have joined them. Marshal left him a message on his new phone but there was no response. The ex-detective thought that was a little odd, not like Buster. Max disassembled Marzia's bed. Marshal removed the bathroom door. A carpenter arrived with a new door for the bathroom. Connor started to load much of the furniture from Marzia's bedroom into the van. It was all destined, in several trips, to Ridley's second-hand shop. When the van was fully loaded, Connor reversed the van out of the garage. Mrs Lewisham watched on.

Once the furniture had been safely returned, Marshal collected his car and followed Connor to the dealership in Bath, to return the van. Conner (or rather Sean McBurney) was about to jump in Marshal's car when an assistant salesman called out to him. He didn't respond at first, as he didn't recognise being called Mr McBurney.

'Just to let you know, we had a telephone call from the police in Bristol. They asked if we had hired out any grey vans, several days after you took your van away on hire,' claimed the assistant.

'Bristol police?' questioned Connor.

'Yes Mr McBurney, we had to give them your name and address. Have you not heard from them? Probably nothing,' said the assistant.

Conner looked horrified. Good job Marshal had the sense to provide a false address when they first booked the van.

Travelling back to Bristol, Connor announced his intended first purchase from his share of the ransom money. He had seen a Subaru BRZ sports car, 6-speed, firestorm red. A demonstrator, with only 6,000 miles on the clock.

'Good grief Connor, how much would that set you back?' exclaimed Marshal.

'Just over £20,000,' replied Connor.

'What would you tell your parents?' asked Marshal. 'They are likely to ask where you acquired that much money. Is it for sale at a Bristol dealership?'

No, it's for sale in a garage in Newbury; I discovered it on the internet,' answered Connor, 'I'm not sure what my parents would say; I would have to tell them I've saved some, and applied for a loan maybe.'

'Seriously Connor, I'm sure it's an amazing motor, but I think you need to set your sights a little lower,' advised Marshal. 'A lad of your age with a car like that, might draw too much attention. Think of the insurance, that could be colossal. I would urge you Connor, to look for a less expensive motor.'

DI Blunt arranged a brief with his team, at the storyboard. A link was added to Joe Billings Junior and Dillon Kelleher, who were in HMP at the same time. DI Blunt asked DC Dolivo if he could compile a list of convicts in the same prison, at the same time that Joe Billings Junior and Dillon Kelleher were imprisoned.

DC Durden explained that they had heard back from the mobile phone company, regarding the four phones used at the Liberty Club. All four are now reported out of service. We haven't been able to trace Alun Muir yet, the guy who purchased twenty phones from the same trader.

DC Dolivo reported that the vehicle dealership in Bath had given them a Sean McBurney as the hirer of a grey van, with a Bristol registration. However, the address they gave for Sean McBurney doesn't exist.

'Sounds rather coincidental,' remarked DI Blunt. 'Bryce and I are going to pay a visit to Dillon Kelleher. Any feedback yet from forensic, on Joe and Chelsea's flat?'

Crime is a Killer

'Not yet Boss,' reported DC Durden.

Marshal dropped Connor off, then went home for a well-deserved rest. Marshal slumped down in his armchair, with a cup of tea and a slice of fruitcake, to listen to his music collection. He was interrupted by a loud knock on his front door. Stood in the doorway was DI Blunt and DS Welles. They showed Marshal their credentials.

'Dillon Kelleher, I am Detective Inspector Marcel Blunt and this is Detective Sergeant Bryce Welles. Do you mind if we come in and ask you a few questions?'

'Not at all,' replied Marshal, and welcomed the two officers into his house.

Marshal offered them refreshment, but they both declined.

'So, how many years were you in the Avon and Somerset Police, Mr Kelleher?' enquired DI Blunt. 'Do you mind if I call you Dillon?'

'Ten years, not at all,' answered Marshal. 'As you must be aware, even at the position of Detective Inspector, the money isn't very remunerative. The temptation to work with a drug cartel was far more financially rewarding.'

'Well, I hope it was all worth it; you certainly have a lovely house,' responded DI Blunt, looking around.

'I paid my penance Inspector,' claimed Marshal.

'How well did you know Stefan Bonanno,' asked DI Blunt.

'I kept well away from him; I considered him a dangerous man. Our relationship was purely business,' was Marshal's response.

'Did you hear, a very nasty business, his daughter Marzia, a singer in a band, was abducted?' questioned DI Blunt.

'Yes, I did hear that,' replied Marshal, 'In fact, I have been following it on the news, as after all, it all happened here in Bristol.'

'Yes, that's right, at the Liberty Club,' responded DI Blunt, 'Do you know the club very well Dillon?'

'Only from years ago, when I was a Detective,' claimed Marshal. 'In my day, there were often skirmishes amongst the youngsters in that club. Thank God, Marzia Bonanno is safe and wasn't harmed. I condemn acts like that; it's the policeman in me, it never goes away.'

'Quite.' replied DI Blunt, 'Stefan Bonanno produced a list for us; the ten most likely men to have abducted his daughter. You were on the list, Dillon.'

Marshal gave out a hearty laugh. 'I'm flattered,' said Marshal, 'Bonanno would have a lot of enemies; quite an achievement to make it on such a list. I see, that's why you are here to ask me questions.'

'He must have thought you would get even with him, as you were discharged from the force, and banged-up as well,' suggested DI Blunt.

'I'm not a man to bear a grudge Inspector. As I see it, Stefan Bonanno is paying his penalty for his crimes; he will be banged-up for a very long time to come,' deliberated Marshal.

'When you were in prison Dillon, do you remember a prisoner called Joe Billings Junior?' asked DI Blunt.

There was a pause, while Marshal contemplated his response. 'Joe Billings Junior, the name rings a bell. I'm struggling to put a face to the name though.'

Crime is a Killer

'Let me help you,' said DS Welles. He reached into his briefcase and produced the police composite drawing of a look-alike Buster.

'Ah, I remember seeing that sketch on TV and thinking it did look a little like an old prison buddy I once knew. We know him as Buster Billings, except he doesn't have as much hair as he does in that sketch,' ridiculed Marshal.

'When was the last time you saw or spoke to Buster Billings, Dillon?' asked DI Blunt.

Another pause. 'It was recently,' answered Marshal, 'He telephoned me, out of the blue.'

'Why would he telephone you?' pressed DI Blunt.

'Just for a chat really,' responded Marshal. 'Reminiscing about prison days. Like me, Buster hasn't found it easy to get work with a criminal record.'

'For just a chat, it was a very long chat,' deduced DI Blunt, 'Twenty-two minutes to be precise.'

Marshal smiled. 'I see you are in possession of Buster's phone.'

'Yes, he is helping us with our enquiries, down at the station,' scoffed DI Blunt. 'So is his girlfriend, Chelsea Lewandowski.'

DS Welles produced a composite sketch of a look-a-like Chelsea, only with long dark hair.

'Do you know Chelsea, Dillon? Have you ever met her?' probed DI Blunt.

'Yes, Chelsea would visit Buster in prison,' replied Marshal, 'Very attractive young lady, I remember. She doesn't look anything like that sketch though; she's blonde.'

At that point DI Blunt attempted to close the discussion.

'You don't think Buster and Chelsea were involved in that abduction, do you?' construed Marshal. 'I can't see it, I'm sorry Inspector. Buster Billings is just a common thief; he's not capable of pulling off a stunt like that, in my opinion.'

'Well, thank you for your opinion Dillon, and thank you for giving up your time today,' responded DI Blunt. 'It's always nice to compare notes with another Detective.'

The officers bid Marshal goodbye and drove off in their police car.

'Slippery character that Dillon Kelleher, I'm not sure I altogether trust him,' remarked DI Blunt to his Sergeant. DS Welles agreed.

CHAPTER 15

The next morning, DCS Dawes-Drake listened to sections of the Buster and Chelsea interviews. DI Blunt's team were positioned around the storyboard, when approached by DCS Dawes-Drake.

'Have we heard from forensics regarding the flat in St Pauls?' asked DCS Dawes-Drake.

'Yes Guv, they didn't find anything that can link either Joe or Chelsea to the abduction. They haven't found any concrete evidence of ransom money in their flat either. They found £570 of mixed bank notes in a drawer in the bedroom. The money would appear to belong to Chelsea, as it was in a chest of drawers, together with ladies' scarves and underwear,' responded DI Blunt. 'Forensics have taken photographs of the serial numbers on the notes; we will be checking if there are any matches to our notes, used for the kidnapping.'

'What do you think Marcel, are we going to have to let them both go?' asked DCS Dawes-Drake.

'Looks that way Guv,' replied DI Blunt. 'We can question Chelsea on the money found, but we don't have enough to charge them on, unless we discover a match on any of those bank notes.'

'What about the ex-policeman?' asked DCS Dawes-Drake. 'Detective Inspector Kelleher. I met him once. City police uncovered a shipment of cannabis; DI Kelleher took charge of the investigation, he seemed to go to the top of the organisation to gain control. A devious character, I thought at the time.'

'Bryce and I paid him a visit at his palatial home in Clifton,' replied DI Blunt. 'Devious is a good description for him. Machiavellian might be another. I would like to put a tail on Mr Kelleher for a few days, see what we can learn. We aim to compile a list of names that were in HMP when he was there, and coincidentally at the same time as Joe Billings Junior.'

'Let's do it Marcel, let's stalk him for a few days,' agreed DCS Dawes-Drake. 'Have you heard from the Met, setting up an interview in London with that Easter fellow?'

'Not yet Guv,' answered DI Blunt. He asked DC Durden if she wouldn't mind giving the Met a little prompt.

At 10.30am, Chelsea was questioned on the money discovered in her bedroom. Chelsea was seething at how the forensic team had searched her flat so rigorously, whilst she was under arrest. Chelsea was adamant the money was hard-earned, dancing at the Megalodon bar.

At 11am, Chelsea and Buster were released from custody.

Yosef Villin took a call on his office telephone, from a Detective Inspector Gail Fishar, of the Hampshire Constabulary. She asked if Yosef had any plans to be in Hampshire; she was keen to obtain character witnesses for the deceased Herman Freud, and a few of his working colleagues, at the time of his tragic death. With the knowledge that Stefan Bonanno was linked to the investigation, Yosef offered to travel to Portsmouth the following day, in order to meet the Inspector.

DI Blunt took a call on his mobile phone from DC Dolivo.

Crime is a Killer

'Boss, I started to plough through the lists of prisoners serving at the same time as Joe Billings & Dillon Kelleher. One name hit me immediately; Niles Easter was serving at the same time.'

'Bingo!' shouted DI Blunt. 'Do the records say what he was banged up for?'

'Yes Boss, robbery of a security van,' came the reply. 'Lissy has confirmed; an interview room at Kensal Green in north London has been allocated, and a Detective Constable Jha, who was involved in the first discussions with Niles Easter, would be there in support.'

DC Dolivo sent a text to DI Blunt, with the post code for Kensal Green police station, mobile number for DC Jha, and the period Niles Easter was imprisoned.

DI Blunt had a new assignment for private detective Aaron Loughty. He gave him the address of Dillon Kelleher.

Buster and Chelsea arrived back at their flat and sat down with a cup of coffee and reflected back on the last two days.

'I never want to go through anything like that again Buster, that was absolutely terrifying,' reflected Chelsea. 'I've decided, I'm not going to work this evening. In fact, I'm thinking of disappearing from Bristol for a while.'

'Where would you go?' asked Buster.

'I might give my sister Morgan a ring,' replied Chelsea. 'See if I can stop with her in Manchester for a few days. I could take a few thousand pounds with me, from the lock-up. Marshal said to spend the money away from Bristol if possible. Do you fancy a few days in Manchester Buster?' she asked.

Buster contemplated the idea, but admitted to Chelsea that he needed to check with Marshal regarding the heist at the jewellers.

Buster went out to his car to retrieve his new mobile phone. He called Marshal to inform him about the arrests. Marshal quite concerningly listened to Buster's dramatic account of his police interview. He questioned Buster on a few of the discussion points, but overall was satisfied that Buster had not divulged anything critical to the operation.

'I would love to talk to Chelsea next Buster, make sure she is not too distressed from the experience,' requested Marshal.

'She wants to get away from Bristol for a while. She's thinking of visiting her sister in Manchester, and laying low,' replied Buster. 'Any more thoughts on the jewellers Marshal?' he asked.

'Well, firstly, I have also had a visit from a Detective Inspector Blunt at my home,' relayed Marshal. 'I wouldn't be surprised if I am the next one in the organisation to receive a tail from the police. I am waiting to hear from Donut; he was going to attempt to break into the boiler building on the roof. If Donut comes back with positive news, I think we should burgle the jewellers quite soon; then we can all lay low then for a while. I favour next Sunday night, early hours of Monday morning. Hopefully at that time, the city centre should be somewhat quieter.'

Marshal spoke to Chelsea next. He was very sympathetic towards her ordeal, but pleased in the way she represented herself in the interview.

Crime is a Killer

DI Blunt drove to Kensal Green police station and met up with DC Jha. They drove to the home of Niles Easter. Niles answered the door; there was a delayed silence. DI Blunt had heard that Niles was a man mountain, but he was quite startled at his sheer size.

'Niles Easter, we are arresting you,' DI Blunt provided the exact same charges that he had relayed to Joe Billings Junior and Chelsea Lewandowski two days previously; he went on to read him his rights.

Niles was dumbstruck, stunned. He glared at DI Blunt. The detective thought he was going to hit him momentarily. The officers chose not to handcuff Niles; they were both relieved he accompanied them to the police car and station voluntarily.

Max was the first to receive his new mobile telephone by registered post. He gave Marshal a call. Marshal explained to Max how Buster and Chelsea had been arrested, and how he had received a visit from a Detective Inspector Blunt.

'It's time to be vigilant,' claimed Marshal, 'Watchful of anything out of the ordinary. This jewellery heist may happen this Sunday evening, early hours of Monday morning, providing Donut can gain entrance without a fuss. We should all go underground for a while afterwards.'

'Spend our £60,000,' suggested Max.

'Quite; well away from Bristol,' replied Marshal.

Chelsea's sister Morgan welcomed Chelsea to stop with her for several days. Her husband Rishi was in the rag-trade, he owned three retail outlets in the north west of England, a small manufacturing and warehouse facility in Bury, an online shopping channel, and manufacturing outlets in India. He was currently travelling in Asia, so Morgan, despite having three children, was delighted to see her younger sister. It had been a long time. It was all arranged for the next day. Buster would drop Chelsea off at Bristol Temple Meads station; Chelsea had a one-way ticket to Piccadilly station Manchester.

DI Blunt took a call from DC Durden just before interviewing Niles Easter. There was no match on the bank notes found in Chelsea's bedroom; plus, the bank admitted that due to the hurried timescales of obtaining half a million pounds of used bank notes, no more than two percent of the serial numbers had been recorded. This was another disappointment for the Detective.

DI Blunt announced the date and time and started the recorded interview with Niles Easter.

'In the room we have Niles Easter. He is represented today by solicitor Guy Fotheringhay. I am Detective Inspector Marcel Blunt, and with me is Detective Constable Daveed Jha.'

DI Blunt questioned Niles on his whereabouts on the evening of the Goddess of Rock concert, and the false address he had provided to the Metropolitan police previously. Niles was adamant, the address on the folded piece of paper, which he took from his wallet, he believed to be where he stayed that night.

'You claimed to be visiting an old friend at this address, by the name of Ajay Sawyers,' declared DI Blunt, 'Tell us Niles, how do you know Ajay Sawyers, perhaps you can provide us with a little background on your relationship with him?'

Crime is a Killer

'We were best friends at college. Ajay's parents were Jamaican; his father got me my first job,' claimed Niles.

'How long since you last saw Ajay? Did you visit anywhere else in Gloucester?' probed DI Blunt.

'Maybe three years,' answered Niles, 'Yes we went for drink in a bar, then back to his house.'

'Does Ajay live alone?' questioned DI Blunt. 'Were there any other friends in the house? What was the name of the bar?'

'No other friends, just Ajay' answered Niles. 'I'm not sure on the name of the bar.' There was a long pause while Niles thought of an answer. 'The Duke, I think it was called The Duke. To be honest I didn't pay much attention at the time.'

'Niles, which college did you and Ajay attend? Do you have Ajay's contact details with you, on your phone?' asked DI Blunt.

'We were at Warnage College in London.' Niles thought that answer was safe submitting, as it was actually true. 'I don't have his contact number, sorry Inspector.'

'You don't have his contact details,' emphasised DI Blunt. 'How did you two get in contact with each other to arrange your visit that weekend?'

'Ajay called me,' claimed Niles. 'I can't believe I didn't record his number.' Niles kept thinking to himself, should the police look on his phone they would soon see Ajay's contact details.

The line of questioning continued; DI Blunt felt that some of Niles' responses were misleading. The Inspector asked Niles for more details on his college days, his knowledge on Marzia's abduction, on his weekend in Gloucester, and the Inspector tried to test his knowledge of Bristol.

'Tell me Niles, you were in prison at the same time as Joe Billings Junior, I believe he is known to you as Buster, and Dillon Kelleher, who you may know as Marshal,' announced DI Blunt.

Niles felt a lump in his throat, at this line of questioning. 'Yes, I knew Buster and Marshal. Why are you asking me about those two guys?' asked Niles.

'Was Stefan Bonanno ever mentioned in prison?' cross-examined DI Blunt.

'Not that I can recall,' answered Niles.

'Stefan Bonanno gave Avon and Somerset Police a list of potential kidnappers of his daughter Marzia. Dillon, (Marshal), was on that list. I wondered if Stefan Bonanno might have come up in conversation, on occasions?'

'No recollection, sorry,' came the reply.

Towards the close of the interview, DI Blunt asked, 'Six different people responded to the composite drawings shown on television, claiming that was you Niles, in Bristol that night. Why do you think so many people thought that was you?'

'I guess it did look a bit like me,' expressed Niles, 'Purely coincidental, I suppose.'

Niles Easter was not charged. After two hours of questioning, he was free to leave. DC Jha gave Niles a lift home.

On leaving Kensal Green station, DI Blunt rang the office. DC Durden answered the phone.

'Lissy, can I ask a favour, can we add Ajay Sawyers to the storyboard, a so-called college best friend of Niles Easter. See if we can find out where he is living now. He might have attended Warnage College in London, around the years of 2001-2004.'

As soon as Niles returned home, he telephoned Ajay Sawyers.

'Ajay, we need to meet. It's urgent. When can we meet?' barked Niles.

'What's up big fella, you're scaring me. I can be home in half an hour,' replied Ajay.

'Great, see you in half hour,' answered Niles.

Niles would have to explain to Ajay how he used his name and false address, to subterfuge the police on his whereabouts on the night of the kidnapping.

That evening, Max paid a visit to the Megalodon bar hoping to see Chelsea. Barman Chubby Bateman explained to Max how Chelsea had telephoned sick. Max could understand why, following the earlier arrest; but he was still quite disappointed not to see Chelsea. A dancer called Bianca danced for him, but it wasn't the same.

The next day Connor and Donut had received their new mobile telephones; each one called Marshal. Connor was asked to hire another van.

'Go to a different dealership this time Connor, not Bath, Sean McBurney,' advised Marshal. 'Hire it either Friday or Saturday.'

Donut had good and bad news for Marshal. The good news was how he managed to unlock the boiler room door on the roof of the jewellers.

'That's brilliant Donut,' responded Marshal. 'We are on for Sunday night, early hours of Monday morning. We can all meet at the safe house at midnight. I have instructed Connor to hire another vehicle. What's the bad news?'

'Patrin will return to Romania with his share of my money on Friday. Alexandru wanted to say goodbye properly to Patrin. He has moved into his caravan,' replied Donut.

'That's a shame Donut, but within a day or two, Alexandru will come back to you,' consoled Marshal. 'Take your mind off of it, think of what treasures we can help ourselves to at the jewellers.'

Yosef drove to Portsmouth to meet with Detective Inspector Gail Fishar. The Inspector was focusing on a line of enquiry on Otto Natchnebel. Herman Freud hired Otto twelve months prior to his tragic death. Otto's position in the company was Stocks and Shares Advisory. DI Fishar was trying to establish if there was a link to Stefan Bonanno. Unfortunately, Yosef was not in a position to supply a character reference for Otto, having met him only once.

THE FOLLOWING SUNDAY EVENING

The five men met at the safe house. They settled in the kitchen at the back of the house, to be less noticeable to neighbours. Mrs Lewisham, when she went to bed at midnight, noticed the downstairs lights were on. She was curious to know whether the Detective had been working away, as she hadn't seen lights on in that house for over a week.

Marshal announced, 'Okay everyone, we are going to rob this jeweller, take as many treasures as we can, and then lay low for a few months. As a gang, we are on the radar of the Avon and Somerset Police department, from our prison days.'

Marshal's partners in crime all loved his confident, dogmatic approach.

'Let's find some treasure,' asserted Max.

Connor pulled up at the entrance to the alleyway. It was a cloudy, dull, dark night. Donut, with his rucksack on his back, climbed up the scaffolding effortlessly. Marshal followed Donut, with less agility. Donut produced the primary key with the red marking; the door unlocked on the first attempt. The two men found their way down to the first floor; Marshal trying to remember where the power circuit breakers, CCTV and laser controls were. Donut and Marshal disconnected all of the controls and ventured down to the ground floor and shop.

It took a while, but Donut used his primary keys to unlock the side door. Max and Buster were waiting there to enter the building.

The men searched the shop and office for keys to unlock the glass cabinets in the shop. This proved to be challenging under flashlight. Donut managed to unlock a storeroom door. In the storeroom was a mix of opened and unopened boxes. Buster and Max started to carry the boxes down the alleyway and into the van. Connor reported no movement of any kind.

'Thank God for that,' commented Max.

Many of the display cases Donut unlocked; those that couldn't be unlocked were smashed open. Marshal was perturbed, smashing the remaining glass cases made too much noise.

'Donut, this safe is not fixed to the floor, it looks heavy, but it's portable. Let's not blow the safe after all,' suggested Marshal. 'Let's get Connor to reverse the van up to the side door. There are five of us, we could drag the safe over to the van. I know some waste land not far from here, we could blow it open there.'

Donut agreed. They arranged for Connor to reverse the van alongside the side door of the property. Dragging the safe from its location, and heaving it into the back of the van proved arduous for the five men. Once the safe was inside the van all five men froze; there were footsteps in the direction of the front of the shop. An inebriated man walked slowly past the alleyway. They all waited until they could no longer hear his footsteps. Donut relocked the side door.

'What about the door on the roof?' asked Donut.

'Leave it,' whispered Max.

'We should really lock it again,' said Marshal, 'only to give the police something more to think about. How did we gain entry? It might buy us more time.'

Donut climbed the scaffolding faster than before, locked the boiler room door, and climbed down again.

Connor, following Marshal's directions, drove the van to wasteland half a mile from Avonmouth Docks. The site was currently being advertised by its owners as an open-air storage facility. It was a derelict site. Marshal advised Connor to reverse the van along a hardcore path to the end.

The five men strenuously unloaded the safe onto a grassy area. Connor drove the van forward, well clear from any explosion.

Crime is a Killer

Donut set the explosives and blasted the safe door open. The explosion echoed. It was as if the echo could be heard two or three times.

'Would you look at these little beauties. They are three of the biggest diamonds I have ever seen,' confessed Marshal.

Max, Donut, Buster and Connor huddled around the ex-detective to take an early peek at the diamonds.

'How are we going to offload them Marshal, and obtain what they are obviously worth?' asked Max.

'I have a good contact in Birmingham, ex-copper, that I believe can help,' professed Marshal. 'It might take a while; Rome wasn't built in a day. I suggest we all go into hiding for a while. I will be in touch with you all regarding our rich pickings tonight.'

Marshal counted the cash in the safe; £2,800.

'In round numbers, that's £500 each, keeping back some cash for the van hire and the journey to Birmingham, to offload the merchandise. Let's get these jewels back to the safe house,' suggested Marshal.

'What about the safe?' asked Connor.

'Let's just leave it,' said Marshal. 'We're hardly going to take it back to the jeweller!'

There was laughter amongst the men. Buster put his arm around Marshal and announced, 'You're the man, Marshal.'

CHAPTER 16

Yosef Villin decided to stay in Portsmouth, to catch up and interview a few employees in the late Herman Freud's office. Janice McCluskey worked adjacent to Otto Natchnebel in the stocks and shares department. Janice confirmed she had handled several transactions on behalf of Stefan Bonanno; she was quite certain that Otto would have emails and transactions on his personal computer from Stefan. Yosef telephoned Detective Inspector Gail Fishar with this information.

'Thank you, Mr Villin,' answered DI Fishar. 'I don't think we will arrest Mr Natchnebel just yet, but we can apply to the magistrates' court for a warrant to seize his computer. We will be in contact, should we come across anything incriminating.'

Marshal reversed his car off his drive, and noticed a black Mercedes parked slightly up the road. Marshal was curious to see if it would follow him, and it did. Marshal smiled and drove into the city centre with his eyes fixed on his rear-view mirror for most of the journey. Marshal was meeting his ex-girlfriend Valesca at the bank. They had planned to open a joint bank account together. Aaron Loughty followed Marshal into a multi-storey car park, parked up nearby, then followed him to the bank. Afterwards, Marshal and Valesca visited a local café for a coffee, then went for a browse around the shops and departmental stores. It was there that Marshal recognised a rather dishevelled, bedraggled character, who was in the car park and in the café; he believed he had identified his tail. Marshal pointed the man out to Valesca.

Crime is a Killer

Chelsea had a shopping day with her sister Morgan while the children were all at school. She bought herself an imposing long dress, matching handbag and shoes. For her sister, a new coat, and matching outfits for the three children. That was the first £1,500 of her share of the ransom money diminished.

Connor had the day off; his priority was searching for a new motor. He took a fancy to a Ford EcoSport 1.5 Titanium Powershift. Petrol, only 13,000 miles on the clock, just under £10,000, at a dealership in Cheltenham. He messaged Marshal with his discovery.

On the Friday, Patrin flew back to Romania. That night, Alexandru moved back into Donut's caravan. Donut was relieved, reassured; he sent a text to Marshal with his welcoming news.

Niles Easter and Ajay Sawyers drove to Gloucester. They were on the search for a house in the city that was not lived in, somewhat run-down. The idea was to create a second fictitious property belonging to Ajay. In reality, it would need to be in the lower property value price range. They drove around districts of Gloucester for an hour without success, when they suddenly spotted a potential house. The paintwork was shabby, the small front garden overgrown, the curtains looked uncared-for; the property was insalubrious.

'Perfect,' declared Niles. 'Let's ask the neighbours about who owns that house.'

The two men parked their car; Niles knocked on a next-door neighbour's house. A middle-aged couple answered the door. They looked terrified at the sheer size of Niles.

Ajay pushed past Niles to explain to the couple that he was looking to buy a run-down house in Gloucester, to renovate as a project. He asked who owned the house next door. The answer he received was encouraging; an elderly man of eighty-seven had died, the house was empty, he had no direct relatives, and a niece was trying to sell it. It had been on the market for over six months. There was a 'For Sale' board outside the house, but one-night youths ran off with it. Ajay made a note of the address, and the estate agent selling the property. He thanked the neighbours, and the two men returned to their car. He never thought to ask the neighbours for the post code of the house.

DI Blunt took a call on his mobile from DC Dolivo. 'Boss, this might be worth following up next; in HMP at the same time as Billings, Kelleher and Easter, were five men from in and around Bristol.' DC Dolivo read the names and their crimes out to the Inspector. There was a stranger amongst the names, a Colin Wicklow, in prison at the same time as the others, serving time for grievous bodily harm. Max, Donut, Connor and Yosef were all on the constable's list.

'I'll storyboard them if you like Boss, and try and find out their current addresses,' suggested DC Dolivo.

'Affirmative, thanks Levi,' replied DI Blunt. 'Can we look at seizing the van that the Bath dealership hired to the contact that we were unable to trace? Get the Governor involved if you have to Levi. It would be good to let forensics crawl all over it for prints and DNA.'

Crime is a Killer

At the back of Marshal's house was a six-foot wooden fence. He would have to scale it for his next mission; he had to escape the eagle-eye of the private detective. A step ladder assisted Marshal on his garden side of the fence; a sheer drop awaited him on the other side. Marshal walked along a footpath, crossed over two roads, to meet Connor, who was waiting for him. Marshal had a large shoulder bag with him, stuffed with used bank notes. The two men reached the safe house, where their hired van was locked in the garage. It contained the merchandise from the jeweller's heist. Connor reversed the van out of the garage, Marshal locked up behind him, and they sped off to Birmingham. Once more, Mrs Lewisham watched on. A different van this time she thought, a white van, with a Money-savers logo on the side.

DI Blunt took a call from DC Durden on his mobile phone.

'Boss, it looks like we may have traced an address for Ajay Sawyers, who attended Warnage College, at the same time as Niles Easter. It's not in Gloucester though, it's in north London, Islington,' reported DC Durden.

'That's interesting,' replied DI Blunt. 'Message me the details Lissy, I could travel up to London tomorrow, have a word with DS Parkin in the Met, see if I could loan DC Jha again for a few hours.'

'Will do, Boss,' acknowledged DC Durden.

Driving up to Birmingham, Connor explained to Marshal how he had seen a Ford EcoSport 1.5 Titanium Powershift; 13,000 miles, just under £10,000.

'Where is the dealership?' asked Marshal.

'Not far, Cheltenham,' answered Connor.

'Go for it, Connor; what else are you going to spend your money on?' replied Marshal. 'Although you might like to start contemplating a possible deposit for a property one day. There will be more money coming our way soon, once we offload all the riches in the back of this wagon.'

Connor was flabbergasted at Marshal's response, 'Go for it!' Marshal gave out a hearty chuckle.

Buster was bored; he despised having to apply for jobs only to be told the vacancy had been filled. He was missing Chelsea; he would phone her several times a day. Buster found himself wandering the streets in Clifton casing up properties to hit.

Marshal and Connor arrived at Geoff's Pawnshop in Dudley. Ex-policeman Geoff Singleton served in Avon & Somerset Police as a Detective Sergeant, in the same department as DI Kelleher. Geoff was the inspiration behind solving what was known at the time as the Bristol Channel murder. Geoff was offered a position of Detective Inspector in the West Midlands Police. Geoff always kept in contact with Marshal, before and after he retired from the police force. Geoff had several retail outlets. A pawnshop and pawnbroker, in Dudley and in Perry Barr, a bric-a-brac shop in Wolverhampton, and a pawnshop jeweller in both Majorca and Ibiza.

Geoff and Marshal gave each other a warm embrace on meeting. Marshal introduced Geoff to Connor.

Crime is a Killer

'Connor is our first-class getaway driver,' declared Marshal. 'We have a van full of treasures for you to take a look at Geoff. Where shall we start?'

'At the back of the shop we have a small empty unit; look out for a silver metal double-door, I will meet you there,' suggested Geoff.

Box by box, sack by sack, the three men emptied the contents of the van into the storeroom at the back of the shop. Bars on the windows, triple lock back door, CCTV, Marshal was impressed with the set-up Geoff had.

'You know Dillon, when you first called me, I thought you would bring me trinkets and gewgaws, and merchandise that might be suitable to sell in my bric-a-brac shop in Wolverhampton, but I have to say, this lot is real quality goods, very sellable.'

Marshal nodded with his approval. Connor wore a curious expression; he had never heard Marshal called Dillon before.

Geoff sifted through the boxes and emptied the sacks; watches, rings, necklaces, bracelets and more, Geoff was quite impressed. He carefully studied the three large diamonds, as Marshal described them.

'I think I will ship these diamonds to Ibiza,' stated Geoff, 'I think they would be worth more there, and probably sell easier than here in the UK.'

Once Geoff had finished examining each item Marshal asked, 'So, are you all right to take all of this merchandise Geoff, and try and sell it all? I have made an itemised inventory for you to cross refer to.'

'Yes, happy to do that Dillon,' replied Geoff. 'The inventory will be most helpful, thank you for that. Some items may sell quicker than others; so, may I suggest I forward on to you at the end of each month, what has sold and the value.'

'That sounds fine Geoff, and are you are still acceptable with a thirty-seventy arrangement?' asked Marshal. 'Here are my bank details to forward any money on to.' Marshal provided Geoff with his new joint account with Valesca.

'Thirty-seventy is fine Dillon,' replied Geoff. 'Thank you for letting me have opportunity to approach the market place with this little lot,'

The two men embraced once again and shook hands on the agreement. Afterwards, Marshal visited branches of his bank in Birmingham city centre and Wolverhampton town centre; he deposited £5,000 of the ransom money in each branch. The money was paid into his new joint account with his ex-girlfriend Valesca.

That evening, Max had an argument with his wife Eleanor. She failed to understand why Max had to keep going to the city centre for a drink. Max stormed out of the house and headed for the Megalodon bar. He was beginning to realise his infatuation with Chelsea was bona fide. Max sat at the bar with a pint of beer, feeling downcast that once again Chelsea wasn't there to dance for him. He wasn't in a hurry to return home, after his row with Eleanor; three pints later, Max decided to ring Buster.

'Hi Buster, it's Max, how are you getting on after your ordeal with the police?'

'Yeah, I'm fine,' said Buster, 'I'm a bit disillusioned, not being able to find work. Might have to rob a few joints for fun.'

Max laughed. 'How's Chelsea?'

Crime is a Killer

'She seems fine; she is stopping with her sister Morgan in Manchester for a few days,' replied Buster.

'Whereabouts in Manchester is that?' asked Max.

'Just outside the city in Salford,' replied Buster.

'I heard she wasn't dancing at the Megalodon, so I did wonder if she was okay,' construed Max.

'How did you know she wasn't dancing at the Megalodon,' snapped Buster.

There was a slight pause, 'Chubby the barman told me,' answered Max.

'Chubby Bateman,' quizzed Buster. 'Were you in the Megalodon then Max?'

Another pause, 'No, not me,' claimed Max, 'Chubby sometimes will come into our shooting range, down at the Activity Centre.'

'Chubby! Shooting! He doesn't seem the type,' challenged Buster.

'I've only ever seen him there on a couple of occasions, he's no regular,' admitted Max. 'So how long will Chelsea stay in Manchester?' he asked.

'No plans at the moment,' declared Buster. 'I've been invited up there, to stay with Chelsea and her sister.'

'Aw, take me with you Buster, I love Manchester; we might get a chance to spend some of our ransom money, away from Bristol,' urged Max. 'I might be able to help you out with Chelsea's sister.'

Buster thought Max's last comment was somewhat weird. 'She's married I'm afraid Max, with three kids.'

'Aw, that's a shame Buster, I imagined her as top totty, just like Chelsea,' came Max's reply.

Afterwards, Buster kept revisiting his conversation with Max; Chubby at the shooting range, questions on Chelsea's return, the possible pairing up with her sister Morgan. All a bit bizarre thought Buster. He decided to phone Chelsea, and portray his conversation with Max. Chelsea put it all down to Max had probably been drinking. She hung up afterwards and thought she had better be honest with Buster soon, on Max's visits to the Megalodon.

The next morning, DI Blunt drove down to Kensal Green police station to meet DC Jha. The two men drove to the apartment of Ajay Sawyers. Ajay's wife Brinda came to the door. Ajay was working, at a local-fishmongers; he had a part time job there. The noise in the apartment of children playing and screaming was noticeable.

'How many children do you have?' asked DI Blunt, politely.

'Five,' came her reply.

The two police officers thanked her and headed off to the fishmongers, where Ajay worked.

'Ajay has been a busy boy,' joked DI Blunt. DC Jha agreed.

The two officers introduced themselves in the shop to Ajay. On the sight of DI Blunt's badge, Ajay's eyes widened like saucers. Ajay asked his boss if he could talk to the two policemen in the shop courtyard. The shop manager looked deeply concerned. There were two grotesque wooden chairs for the policemen to sit on; Ajay perched on a stack of wooden crates.

'Mr Sawyers, how well do you know a Niles Easter?' questioned DI Blunt.

Crime is a Killer

Ajay had anticipated this line of questioning. 'He was a good friend to me, when I was at college,' came his reply.

'Warnage College,' confirmed DI Blunt. 'Have you always lived in London?'

'Yes, Warnage College, and yes, I have always lived in London,' answered Ajay.

'So, you don't live in Gloucester then,' sprung DI Blunt.

'Ah yes Gloucester,' retorted Ajay. I don't live in Gloucester, Inspector, but I have bought a house there.

DI Blunt read out the address provided by Niles Easter.

'Nah, that's not the address,' avowed Ajay. He provided the Inspector with the address from their visit, the day before.

'How long have you owned this property?' enquired DI Blunt.

'Picked up the keys,' there was a pause, 'The week before Niles came to visit me.'

'So, Niles came to this address when?' quizzed DI Blunt.

Ajay contemplated for quite some time, then he gave the Inspector the weekend date, of the abduction.

'I don't mean to be disrespectful Mr Sawyers, but you live in an apartment, with your wife and five children, yet you can buy a house in Gloucester; how come?' questioned DI Blunt.

'I have been saving for a deposit on a house for many years Inspector, but please don't say anything to my wife Brinda. She doesn't know about the house yet; I want to surprise her. It is a run-down property, an old man of eighty-seven lived there and died,' answered Ajay with an arrogance.

'Niles Easter told us that you went to a pub that weekend, but he couldn't remember the pub's name. Can you remember which pub it was?' enquired DI Blunt.

Fortunately, for the cover-up story, Ajay remembered what Niles had told him; 'It was The Duke, I think Inspector.'

Ajay's account of that weekend matched Niles Easter's account, however the Inspector was not convinced; it was as if the two of them had colluded. After the interview, Ajay returned to his fish counter. DI Blunt and DC Jha returned to Kensal Green police station.

DI Blunt did not drive directly back to Bristol, he diverted up the M5 motorway to Gloucester. He plugged the address Ajay had provided into his satnav. The Inspector parked directly outside the property. It looked dilapidated, just as Ajay Sawyers had described, thought the Inspector. He ventured from his vehicle and approached a neighbour on the opposite side of the road.

'Excuse me sir, do you know who lives in that house?' asked DI Blunt, pointing at the shabby house opposite.

'No one lives there, officer,' said the neighbour. 'Old Albert did live there, but he died, he was eighty-seven.'

That's interesting, thought the Inspector; that matched what Ajay Sawyers had said. How would he know that level of detail?

'So, it must be for sale, or perhaps even sold?' questioned DI Blunt.

'Not sure,' replied the neighbour, 'Albert didn't appear to have any family, or friends; no one ever came to visit him.'

Crime is a Killer

'Thank you,' replied DI Blunt, 'One last question if I may, can you tell me in which direction is a public house called The Duke?'

'The Duke,' contemplated the neighbour. 'I don't know of any pub around here called The Duke; sorry Officer.'

DI Blunt asked DC Durden if she could find a public house in Gloucester called The Duke. The Constable conducted an internet search; she couldn't find a pub by that name, not in Gloucester.

The following morning, Marshal and Valesca sat in his kitchen eating breakfast. It was an opportunity for Marshal to catch up on some local news. In reading the Bristol Post, he started to read an article with great interest. For the month of January, there was to be an art exhibition of a difference; street art. A top Argentinian street artist would exhibit fifteen works of art. How apt, thought Marshal, for such an exhibition to come to Bristol; world famous for the city's own street art.

He read the article to Valesca; it was the works of Argentinian Felipe Mar Arrazquito. The Post referred to Filipe as one of the top ten street artists in the world. The exhibition would take place in the Mission Hut.

'Where's the Mission Hut?' asked Valesca.

'It's that old corrugated tin hut that sits on the side of the River Avon, on the Cumberland Road near Wapping Wharf,' answered Marshal.' I've known them hold the odd fete, jamboree and convention there, but never an exhibition on this scale.'

CHAPTER 17

Ajay Sawyer arranged to meet Niles Easter at a local café near the fishmongers where he worked. Ajay was keen to update Niles on his conversation with the police.

'Ajay, sorry mate but I have to say, you reek of fish,' was the greeting he received from Niles.

Ajay described how the discussion had evolved with Detective Inspector Blunt.

'That seemed to go to plan Ajay,' replied Niles. 'Sounds as if it was definitely worth travelling across to Gloucester the day before.'

'What if the police check out there is no Duke pub nearby?' asked Ajay. 'What if they find out the house in Gloucester is still for sale?'

'I will check on the Internet,' confirmed Niles. 'Now we know the street name, we can find out what the nearest pub is called. A simple mistake, they can't charge us for making a mistake Ajay. As for the house, we can say you were genuinely interested in buying the property. Having made the journey to Gloucester, we simply broke into the house to stay there the night.'

'So, would that be a breaking and entry charge?' quizzed Ajay.

'Don't worry Ajay, that won't stick,' declared Niles, with an air of confidence. 'Squatters for just one night.'

DI Fishar and DC Harris raided the office of Otto Natchnebel and confiscated his laptop computer. Leading up to that, the Inspector had a heated conversation with the company's management, over the warrant produced without their knowledge. Janice McCluskey looked on in anguish; it was probably her conversation with Yosef Villin that led to this raid. Otto Natchnebel looked agitated, flustered, but he was not arrested.

DI Blunt was in the office, there was a small gathering at the storyboards. The enquiry was growing, consequently there was a need for a second storyboard. DC Dolivo provided three addresses of ex-prisoners in HMP at the same time of Joe, Dillon and Niles, with two more to ascertain. Yosef Villin, Colin Wicklow and Max Currigan. DC Durden confirmed that a forensic team were on route to the van dealership in Bath. She also reported that the manager of the dealership was not particularly helpful and quite sceptical.

DI Blunt and DS Welles kicked off their ex-convict roundup by visiting Yosef Villin, at his home. His wife Leah answered the door; she was very apologetic. She explained how Yosef had some business to attend to down in Hampshire.

'Do you know when Yosef is likely to return home?' asked DI Blunt.

'Yes, I am expecting him home tomorrow,' came her reply, 'Can I ask what this is all about Inspector?'

'We just wanted to talk to your husband about someone he might have known when he was in prison Mrs Villin, we can call again tomorrow, that's not a problem,' indicated DI Blunt.

On route to Colin Wicklow's home, DI Blunt took a call from DCS Dawes-Drake.

'Any luck with the house calls Marcel?' asked DCS Dawes-Drake.'

'Not yet Guv, the first call was to Yosef Villin, sadly he wasn't home, we need to return there tomorrow. We are on our way to a second call, a Colin Wicklow.'

'Okay, good luck,' responded DCS Dawes-Drake. 'I have been revisiting the statements of Marzia Bonanno. She said one of the abductors, the one with the superhero face mask, had a strong Bristol accent; another had a deep voice, African, almost American twang. We could ask Marzia if she would attend a voice recognition line-up. I'm sure she would agree following the ordeal she went through. Niles Easter's voice might not be so easy to replicate; the local Bristol accent might be more straightforward. You could ask DC Dolivo to stand in for starters.'

'That's a good idea Guv,' replied DI Blunt. 'So, if we set up several short recordings of say, three other Bristol accents, and throw in a few short recordings from the Joe Billings Junior interview.'

'That should work Marcel,' stated DCS Dawes-Drake. 'You shouldn't have any trouble finding a few Bristolians in Bridewell police station.'

Both men laughed.

DI Blunt and DS Welles arrived at the home of Colin Wicklow. Colin was irritated, vexed by receiving a visit from two police officers.

'Mr Wicklow, we would just like to ask you a few questions concerning prisoners you may have come across when you served in HMP,' requested DI Blunt. 'May we come in?'

Crime is a Killer

Colin Wicklow reluctantly asked the two officers into his home.

'Do you live here on your own, Mr Wicklow?' asked DI Blunt.

'None of your business,' came his indignant reply, 'Let's get to the point.'

'We would like to know what you may know about the following fellow prisoners.' DS Welles slowly read out seven names, six from the Bristol area, plus Niles Easter.

Colin Wicklow shook his head at every name read. He didn't appear to know any of them by name.

DI Blunt thought that rather strange. DS Welles showed Colin the composite sketch of Niles Easter.

'Yes, I recognise him, big bastard he was,' replied Colin. 'I stayed well out of his way.'

DS Welles showed him the composite drawing of Joe Billings Junior.

'He looks facially like a prisoner I was paired up with on toilet duties once, he was going bald though,' came Colin's response.

'We don't have any more sketches to show you, Mr Wicklow. I'm surprised you don't recognise any of the names read earlier,' stated DI Blunt.

'Inspector, here is how it is,' Colin held his breath for a second before he replied, 'I am gay. You know what can happen to gays sometimes in prison, Inspector. I kept myself very much to myself. I was only serving a six-month sentence; not too long to keep a low profile and stay out of trouble. Now is there anything else I can help you with today Inspector?'

DI Blunt admitted no, with a shake of the head. The two police officers thanked Colin for his time and left.

Marshal decided to investigate further the forthcoming street art exhibition of Filipe Mar Arrazquito. Fifteen works of art, all on six-feet high, four-feet width canvas. Four of the artworks had been sold. They would be mounted on a central custom-built roundabout, to be displayed at the core focal point of the exhibition. Marshal studied each piece of artwork; he found the listing and photographs were extremely interesting. Marshal discovered a listing, translating each piece of art, from Argentinian to English;

1. Lost Woman.
2. Masked Monkey Healthcare - SOLD.
3. Maniac Moon.
4. Girl with a Drill.
5. Dark Money – SOLD.
6. Heavenly Carpet Ride.
7. Creatures Last Tango – SOLD.
8. Cemetery Dogs.
9. The Mouse with the Gun.
10. Hand of Fear.
11. Cat Alley.
12. Walking Dead.
13. Smoking Kills.
14. Sprung from Jail – SOLD.
15. Dragon on Fire.

Marshal was curious to learn more about the works of art that had already sold. The price range varied from 95 million to 190 million Argentine Pesos; the approximate equivalent of British pounds sterling of £750,000 to £1,500,000. Marshal scrolled several websites to try and establish who the buyers might be; many were in Spanish, so his patience was examined. Then he found an article in a Buenos Aires link to an online website, called Sparkr. Here he found the four buyers to date. Caleb Tchaikovsky, listed as a Russian businessman; Marshal would not be aware of his connection with Stefan Bonanno. Santiago Apraiz, listed as an Argentinian shipping entrepreneur. Valentina Cunchillos, listed as the head of a municipality healthcare organisation, in Argentina. When Marshal read the fourth buyer, he could not believe his eyes. It was Stefan Bonanno, there was no listing of his background, just businessman.

Marshal had to tell someone of his findings, so he phoned his ex-girlfriend Valesca. 'Hi honey, guess what I have just discovered, I can't believe it.'

'Go on Dillon, go ahead and surprise me,' answered Valesca.

'Remember I told you that of the total of Filipe Mar Arrazquito's art collection, four had been sold,' Marshal deliberately paused the conversation for effect.

'Yes,' came Valesca's response, trying to anticipate where the conversation was heading.

'One of the buyers is only Stefan Bonanno,' announced Marshal, 'He would have paid anything between £750,000 to £1.5 million pounds for his piece of street art.'

'I'm not sure where this is taking us,' said Valesca cautiously.

'When we case the Mission Hut, we have to help ourselves to those four works of art,' said Marshal gleefully.

Following his conversation with Valesca, Marshal spent several more hours reading up on Filipe Mar as a person, and his artwork. He deduced for his own satisfaction that the head of healthcare had bought 'Masked Monkey

Healthcare'; The Russian had bought 'Dark Money'; the shipping entrepreneur had bought 'Creatures Last Tango'; and finally, Stefan Bonanno would have bought 'Sprung from Jail'. How ostentatious of him, thought Marshal.

DI Blunt and DC Welles arrived at the home of Max Currigan. They introduced themselves, showing their police credentials.

'Mr Currigan, we have a few questions concerning a few men you may have come across when you were in HMP,' declared DI Blunt, 'May we come in?'

'Can't I answer these few questions stood here on the doorstep? My wife and boy are in the house,' replied Max with a certain arrogance.

'Yes, if you prefer, Mr Currigan,' answered DI Blunt. 'I see you were charged for possessing a loaded weapon at a demonstration in the city centre.'

DI Blunt's intention was to introduce weaponry into the conversation, bearing in mind one of the abductors had a gun.

'Yes, that's correct,' replied Max. 'But as I explained in court at the time, I didn't realise it was loaded. I served time for that offence; is that the only reason why you are here?'

'No Mr Currigan, we were curious to know if you have managed to find work in the local area,' replied DI Blunt.

'Yes, thank you, I have a job at the Activity Centre, on the shooting range,' answered Max.

'Sounds like you like playing with guns, Mr Currigan,' came DI Blunt's response.

Crime is a Killer

'That's three questions, do you have any more?' barked Max.

'Just a few,' DI Blunt replied. 'Do you recall from your time in prison, a Joe Billings Junior, or a Dillon Kelleher?'

'No' was Max's blunt reply.

'Ah, you may have known them possibly under different names; how about Buster and Marshal?' asked DI Blunt.

'Yes, I met those two characters inside,' confirmed Max.

'Have you had chance to meet or talk to either of them since your release?' enquired DI Blunt.

'Why would I?' asked Max. 'Prison isn't actually the best place to make friends, Inspector.'

'No, quite right,' replied DI Blunt. 'Did you ever hear the name Stefan Bonanno?'

'Wasn't he on the news recently, wasn't his daughter kidnapped?' asked Max.

'Yes, that's right. Did you follow the news on the kidnapping at the time, Mr Currigan? Did you ever hear his name spoken in prison?' questioned DI Blunt.

'Only on TV. Now you come to mention it, wasn't he the head of the drugs cartel that got Marshal banged up?' responded Max.

'So did Marshal talk to you regarding Stefan Bonanno on a regular basis?' enquired DI Blunt.

'No, just the once, when I asked him why he was in prison,' came the deceitful answer of Max. 'Is there anything else I can help you with, I'm freezing my nuts off stood here talking to you two.'

'One final question and we will leave you in peace, Mr Currigan. Do you happen to have a sawed-off shotgun at home?' questioned DI Blunt.

'No, I don't Inspector,' lied Max. 'I have a young boy at home, why would I keep a gun in my house?'

The two officers thanked Max for his time. As they walked up the front garden path toward their police car, DI Blunt turned and asked,

'Mr Currigan, does the name Chelsea Lewandowski mean anything to you?'

Max thought for a moment. 'The only Chelsea I knew of, was Buster's girlfriend, who came to visit him in prison a few times. Drop dead gorgeous blonde, is that her?'

'Yes, that's her, thank you Mr Currigan.'

Max closed his front door and thought he should take his personal weaponry to work and hide them, in case the police obtained a search warrant.

DI Blunt was convinced Max Currigan knew far more than he was letting on. He announced to DS Welles of his intention to apply for a search warrant of Max Currigan's home.

Buster visited the Megalodon bar that evening. Buster knew most of the dancers, so there was a lot of different company for Buster to talk to while Chelsea was staying at her sisters. Chelsea's close friend, Hannah, wanted to know when she would be back in Bristol. Chubby Bateman came on shift for bar work at 9pm.

'I didn't realise you went to the shooting range Chubby,' said Buster.

Crime is a Killer

'Shooting range, what shooting range?' asked Chubby.

'Down the Activity Centre,' verified Buster.

'Activity Centre, I've never set foot in there in my life,' replied Chubby. 'I hate shooting; when I was a kid my uncle took me rabbit shooting. I thought I had broken my shoulder with the rifle buttstock. Never went shooting again.'

Buster described Max to Chubby, claiming that it was Max that told him about the shooting range.

'Sounds like one of the characters that visits this bar,' suggested Chubby. 'In fact, this fella I'm thinking of likes to ask your Chelsea to dance for him.'

'How often have you seen him in here? How often did he ask Chelsea to dance for him?' raged Buster.

'I don't know, half a dozen times, dozen or more dances, I suppose. You tend to watch the punters and how they behave, Buster. You don't count them in,' answered Chubby.

Buster was seething. He finished off his drink, said goodbye to Chubby, went to his car and phoned Chelsea. He explained to her how Max lied about Chubby visiting the shooting range, how many times Chubby thought he had seen Max in the Megalodon, and approximately how many dances she had performed for Max.

'I wanted to tell you Buster, but I was scared,' responded Chelsea. 'Scared because of who it was, Max.'

'How could you agree to dance for him Chelsea, Max of all people,' howled Buster.

'Buster, it's my job to dance with customers, you know that. You haven't got jealous before,' uttered Chelsea.

'Yeah, but Max. I'll kill him,' threatened Buster.

'Buster, don't do anything ………' before Chelsea had said the word 'stupid,' Buster had hung up the phone.

His next call was to Max.

'Buster, good to hear from you.' Max walked into a different room, away from his wife Eleanor's ability to hear.

'That was an outright lie you told me about Chubby Bateman, Max. I found out from Chubby, he has never set foot in your shooting range. You knew Chelsea wasn't working at the Megalodon because you were visiting the bar on a regular basis, to stalk Chelsea I suspect,' implied Buster.

'How is Chelsea?' asked Max audaciously.

'You've got to stay away from my Chelsea, Max, do you understand?' growled Buster.

'Buster, going into a bar for a few drinks and watching sexy ladies pole dance is just a bit of fun; you need to lighten up a little Buster,' responded Max.

'It was much, much more than just watching the dancers,' retaliated Buster, 'I have spoken with Chelsea, you stalked her, and pleaded with her to dance for you, many times. Go near her again Max, and I'll either put you in hospital, or in a wooden overcoat.'

'Buster, let's not do this over the phone,' replied Max, 'Give me your address, I'll come and pick you up. We can have a man-to-man chat, and sort this silly nonsense out.'

Buster didn't trust Max at all; he wondered why he had suggested a man-to-man chat. He drove back to his flat in St Pauls; in a bedroom drawer was to be his defence, an iron, four-fingered knuckle duster. Buster didn't have to wait very long before Max had arrived at his flat. Max drove out of Bristol, toward the River Severn. The car was silent for the entire journey. Eventually they reached Whale Wharf on the banks of the Severn. It was late evening by now, and quite dark, just a new moon appearing now and again, with a break in the clouds. Max parked the car near the public footpath and invited Buster to walk the wharf with him. Buster didn't trust Max; when he wasn't looking, he slipped his fingers on his right hand into the knuckle duster.

As the two men walked slowly down the wharf, in the direction of the Severn Bridge, Max tried to soften the mood a little.

'I like to come here for moments of tranquillity, although on a windy day it can be mind-blowing,' implied Max. 'Do you know why it is called Whale Wharf, Buster?'

'No,' came an abrasive reply.

'In the late nineteenth century, a sixty-eight-foot whale was beached here on the river bank and died,' declared Max.

'Let's get back to talking about Chelsea,' interrupted Buster, 'That's why we are here, on a cold dark night.'

'Buster, I am thinking of leaving my wife,' exclaimed Max. 'This would make me single again. I would have more opportunity to become intimate with Chelsea.'

Buster stopped in his tracks. 'I told you Max, not to go near her, she is my girlfriend.'

'But Buster, she excites me, she turns me on. I am infatuated with her, I can't stay away from her, sorry Buster,'

'You have to stay away,' screamed Buster. He threw a punch at Max, with his knuckle duster hand. Max hit the grass footpath floor hard.

There was a shot. Max fired a Glock 19, 9mm hand gun, from his coat pocket. Buster fell to the floor holding his stomach. Max rose to his feet, took the gun from his pocket and fired a second shot into Buster's chest. He died instantly.

CHAPTER 18

Max stood over Buster's dead body for several minutes. He tried to reflect back on what had just happened. Max was in a lot of pain; he looked down at Buster's hand and saw the knuckle duster. So that's why my jaw hurts so much, he thought. He would have to dispose of the body; the River Severn being the obvious place to conceal Buster's body. Max searched Buster's pockets; he removed two mobile phones, a watch, and a wallet. After removing a solitary ten-pound note from Buster's wallet, he threw the wallet, watch and the mobile phones into the River Severn.

Nearby, Max spotted a pile of household rubbish that had been fly-tipped. Max had seen it a few days earlier; he was pleased to see that the City Council hadn't had a chance to clear it. There was a wooden door, a bedstead, a stone sink with taps and pipework attached. The door would be ideal to float Buster's body out towards the centre of the river, thought Max. Max took a pair of latex gloves from his coat pocket and put them on. He carried the door to the edge of the river; another bonus thought Max; the tide was in. He dragged Buster onto the door; it is true what they say about dead bodies being a dead weight, thought Max. He would need something heavy to submerge Buster to the bottom of the river. That sink, thought Max, perfect. Max carried the sink over to the door and placed it on Buster's blood covered chest. He would need something to tie the sink to the body. He mooched amongst the fly-tipped rubbish; a coiled-up washing line, perfect again. He untied the line from two posts, and then secured the line to the sink pipework and to both of Buster's arms and legs.

Max left his shoes, watch, phone and wallet on the river bank, and edged the door slowly into the river. Swimming alongside the door, he tried to reach the middle of the river, but there was an undercurrent which took Max and the door many yards upstream. Max was growing tired; his jaw was very painful. He decided to tip the door slowly, so that Buster's body would slide off the door, and into the river. Buster's body slowly submerged into the River Severn. A few air bubbles appeared; Max was not expecting to see bubbles in the slightly moonlit river.

Max swam back to the riverbank with one hand on the door handle. Was that blood on the door? He turned the door over, hoping that the water would wash it away. He left the door floating in the river. Max returned to his vehicle, and took off most of his soaking wet clothes. He drove home in his underwear and shoes. Back at his home, Max laid his wet clothes out in his garage. Now naked, Max crept into his kitchen to try and find some painkillers.

The next morning, in Hampshire, Otto Natchnebel was arrested for the murder of Herman Freud. The police arrested him at his office; his work colleagues looked on in total dismay.

Max Currigan rose early that morning to set off to work. He put the clothes from the garage into the boot of his car. He noticed blood stains on his combat jacket. He would have to try and burn that jacket and remaining clothes, he thought. Max had already packed his car boot with his personal arsenal of weapons and ammunition. He was taking it all to the Activity Centre, where he worked.

Crime is a Killer

Max hoped that he had outmanoeuvred his wife on this occasion, by hiding his bespattered clothing. He drove to work cautiously, not wanting to draw attention to himself. Max had another stroke of luck; his boss was not at work that day. He was alone on the shooting range, too early in the day for customers. There was a disused outbuilding on the range. Max stowed away his personal arsenal in the roof space of the building. He lit a small bonfire in a garden incinerator bin, and burnt his blood-stained jacket and remaining clothes. Max thought, after his shift at the shooting range, he would go straight to the accident and emergency department of Southmead Hospital; he feared that Buster might have broken his jaw.

DI Blunt held a review at the storyboards. DC Dolivo provided the Inspector with the address of ex-inmate Connor Jackson. So far, they had drawn a blank with Lonut Coltescu. The prison records had him living in Avonmouth at a demolition site. The Inland Revenue had him on record as living on a hop farm, in Worcestershire. DC Dolivo pointed out Lonut was originally an immigrant from Romania.

'Let's not spend too much time then on this individual,' instructed DI Blunt. 'We can visit Connor Jackson and revisit Yosef Villin first, and see where that takes us.'

DC Durden confirmed they were expecting the search warrant for Max Currigan's property later that day.

'Fantastic,' responded DI Blunt. 'Lissy, let me know as soon as it arrives; we can pay another visit to Mr Currigan.'

DS Welles confirmed the results of the forensic search on the van from the Bath dealership. Marzia's fingerprints, hair and DNA were evident in the back of the vehicle. There was no match found to Joe Billings Junior or Chelsea Lewandowski in the van. The forensic team did stress in their report, the vast number of prints throughout the vehicle.

Disappointed by this result, DI Blunt and DS Welles planned their next visit, the home of Connor Jackson.

Chelsea's sister Morgan, packed the children off to school, and sat down with Chelsea for an exotic fruit breakfast. Chelsea was a little concerned, she hadn't heard from Buster the night before; he would often try to call her last thing at night.

DI Blunt and DS Welles called at the home of Connor Jackson. Connor happened to be working that day; his father answered the door.

'What's all this about Inspector?' asked Mr Jackson, 'Has Connor been speeding again, in his new car?'

'No,' replied DI Blunt, 'Nothing like that. We would like to ask him a few questions about someone he might have met in HMP. Did you say Connor has a new car?'

'Yes, that little red number parked over there,' Mr Jackson pointed over to the car.

'A Ford EcoSport 1.5 Titanium Powershift, very nice,' expressed DS Welles.

'I don't know where these kids of today get their money from, Connor is only a part-time delivery driver,' voiced Mr Jackson.

Both men thanked Mr Jackson and promised to call back later that evening.

Crime is a Killer

Marshal and his ex-girlfriend Valesca drove to a bank in Newport, then on to a bank in Cardiff, to deposit £5,000 in to each bank, in to their new, joint bank account. Afterwards, they parked up near Wapping Wharf. Marshal was keen to take a close look at the Mission Hut. Marshal tapped the back corrugated wall with his hand; it sounded very hollow.

'Do you know Valesca, it wouldn't take much to knock a big hole in that back wall,' declared Marshal.

There was a small car park behind the hut. At low-tide a set of concrete steps lead down to the River Avon. It was open to the Cumberland Road, no restrictive access. There was only one entrance, on the roadside. Marshal peered through two of the hut's windows; the building was empty, capacious in appearance. The hut had a stone-built chimney in the centre of the building, with a wood burning stove inside. I guess that would be lit in January when the art exhibition would take place, thought Marshal. He then pondered on the positioning of this so-called central, custom-built roundabout the paintings would be mounted on, that had been sold. Marshal offered to buy Valesca a drink in a nearby pub, and start the planning of operation, 'Getaway Again'.

DI Blunt and DS Welles visited the home of Yosef Villin. They received a very civilised reception with tea, coffee and Victoria sponge cake. Yosef remembered most of the names from his prison encounter; Niles, Max, Connor, Dillon, the latter he remembered having a conversation on how he acquired the title of Marshal. When questioned on the name of Stefan Bonanno, Yosef nodded and answered.

'Oh yes, I have certainly heard of Stefan Bonanno. Marshal may have mentioned him, I'm not terribly sure now. As for the kidnapping, at the time I didn't put two and two together, with Stefan being the girl's father, but recently Bonanno has been connected to the murder of one of my highly thought of financial controllers, Herman Freud.'

DI Blunt looked at Yosef with a scowling expression, 'You know of this?'

'Yes Inspector,' replied Yosef, 'I have been helping the Hampshire police with their enquiries. Herman hired a stocks and shares broker called Otto Natchnebel. The Hampshire police had confiscated Otto's computer; they have found evidence linking Bonanno to the murder. Otto Natchnebel was arrested for the murder of poor Herman, only this morning.'

DI Blunt was astounded with this news. It seemed to kill off his line of questioning with Yosef Villin. DI Blunt needed to get his head around what he had just heard. The Inspector thanked Mr and Mrs Villin for their time and hospitality, and the two officers left and went about their duty.

In the nearby pub, Marshal ordered a pint of craft lager, while Valesca ordered an Orgasm cocktail. They discussed breaking into the Mission Hut; there was an air of confidence coming from Marshal on that task. The getaway, they discussed through in some detail. The conclusion was to make off with the artwork, by boat, up the River Avon, toward the River Severn.

'I could chat to Chadd Aitken; he's a good friend,' suggested Marshal. 'Chadd helped us with a manoeuvre, that allowed us to kidnap Marzia.' Marshal had earlier confided in Valesca, over the kidnapping.

'Chadd has a spacious river cruiser moored locally somewhere,' announced Marshal, 'It has a double cabin, HiLine spec head room. We could cut Chadd in to a share of the fortune that these works of art are likely to fetch. All we need is a boatyard on the Severn, where we can off-load all of the artwork.'

'I might possibly be able to help you there, Marshal,' confessed Valesca. 'My cousin Robbie has a boatyard, where the River Severn meets the River Wye, near Chepstow. He has a six-berth sea cruiser; he often takes it out into the Bristol Channel in the summer months. He once explained to me that the River Wye estuary is tidal.'

This gained Marshal's attention, 'How big is it though?'

'It's big,' answered Valesca, 'You would get two boats of that size in there easy.'

'What if we can't get Chadd on board; do you think your cousin Robbie would come in with us?' asked Marshal.

'Not sure,' hesitated Valesca, 'He's as straight as a die.'

DI Blunt and DC Dolivo returned to the home of Connor Jackson, while DS Welles and a new recruit to the department, DC Davidson visited the home of Max Currigan, with a search warrant to seek out any weaponry or ammunition. This really stressed Max's wife Eleanor.

Connor came to the front door. DI Blunt preferred a doorstep discussion on this occasion. Connor was read the names of seven prisoners from his time in HMP. Connor professed to know Joe (Buster), Niles, Yosef, Lonut and Max; he denied knowing Colin Wicklow and Dillon Kelleher.

'What about Stefan Bonanno?' enquired DI Blunt.

Connor shook his head, 'Never heard of him.'

'Try Marzia Bonanno,' came the Inspector's response.

Connor shook his head once again.

'Don't tell me you haven't heard of the young girl who was kidnapped recently, and held captive in Bristol,' retorted DI Blunt.

'Oh, yes, I heard about that; was that her name?' questioned Connor.

'That gleaming red Ford motor parked over there, I understand belongs to you Connor,' construed DI Blunt.

Connor didn't answer; he gave the Inspector a nod of the head. Connor wondered how the Inspector knew that was his car.

'How can a young man like you, as a part time delivery driver, afford a car like that?' probed DI Blunt.

'Savings,' came Connor's reply, 'Part loan.' Connor was shocked that the Inspector knew his line of work.

'Which loan company did you borrow from?' came a further probing question from the Inspector.

'You may be the police, but I don't see that as any of your business,' snapped Connor.

'Don't worry Connor, we can obtain that information from the National Crime Agency,' replied DI Blunt.

Connor didn't know if the Inspector was bluffing or not; his throat went suddenly dry. At that point, DI Blunt thanked Connor for his time, and walked back to their police car. The Inspector stopped and inspected Connor's vehicle. He walked around it; he even crouched down to look inside the vehicle. This was all for Connor's benefit. Connor watched on from the glass window in his front door.

On returning to the police car, DI Blunt had a message from Aaron Loughty. The Inspector returned his call. The private detective was not finding it easy to tail Dillon Kelleher. Aaron suggested offering Dillon a short-term contract of detective work. That way, he might be able to keep tabs on the ex-policeman that much easier. DI Blunt thought that was a good idea.

The next morning, DI Blunt's team met at the storyboards. DC Durden started with news that Marzia Bonanno had agreed to attend a voice line-up. DC Dolivo announced that the house in Gloucester that Ajay Sawyers claimed to own was for sale, and he had added the estate agent to one of the storyboards. DS Welles informed the team that the gun search at Max Currigan's home had proven negative. Then he announced better news; Dr Weatherby from forensics had called; he has discovered a DNA match on the wig recovered from the Liberty Club, with Joe Billings Junior.

'Bingo,' shouted DI Blunt; that happened to be one of his favourite expressions, when something went well. 'Are we sure? What did Dr Weatherby say?'

'Dr Weatherby explained that cut or shed hair doesn't contain any nuclear DNA; he indicated there were several loose hairs found in the wig.' DS Welles went on to explain, 'However, there were three hairs with follicles at the base of the hair, which contain cellular material rich in DNA. Those hairs matched Joe Billings Junior's DNA.'

'Then we can re-arrest Billings Junior, brilliant,' exclaimed DI Blunt. 'Bryce, we'll go and read him his rights next. Afterwards, maybe you could travel up to Gloucester and check with that estate agent, who has viewed that property. I'd like to bet that Ajay Sawyers won't be one of them. Lissy, how are we getting on with the Bristol accent recordings?'

'Just one more to record Boss, a Sergeant Cummings has offered to participate,' reported DC Durden.

'Great, if this proves positive and Marzia identifies the voice of Joe Billings, with the DNA as well, it's going to be a long time in a police cell for Mr Billings,' announced DI Blunt.

The Inspector breezed past DCS Dawes-Drake's office, with the good news.

For Chelsea it was another day with no word from Buster. She was starting to worry, especially after hearing him so angry with Max. She had no way of contacting Max since the mobile telephones used for the kidnapping had all been destroyed. Chelsea announced to her sister that she had better head back to Bristol, something was horribly wrong.

DI Blunt and DS Welles arrived at Buster and Chelsea's flat in St Pauls, but no one was home. That frustrated DI Blunt; he was anxious to make that second arrest.

DS Welles drove on to Gloucester to meet the estate agent selling the dilapidated property. The agent confirmed that Ajay Sawyers had not made contact, and had not viewed the property. DS Welles relayed this information to DI Blunt, it was how he suspected. He might have to ask the officers in the Met to make further calls on Ajay Sawyers and Niles Easter.

DI Blunt and DC Dolivo returned to Buster and Chelsea's flat later that day, but once again no one was home. They proceeded on to the Megalodon bar; DI Blunt had hoped to see Chelsea there. The Inspector was told that Chelsea hadn't been seen at the bar for several days; there was no explanation on her whereabouts either. DI Blunt feared that Chelsea and Joe Billings might have absconded somewhere with their share of the ransom money.

Marshal was impressed with the Argentinian online website, Sparkr. Their newsfeed was in both Spanish and English and quite informative, regarding the street art exhibition, soon to be in Bristol. The fifteen works of art had arrived in the UK and were stored in a secret location.

The artist Filipe Mar Arrazquito was due to arrive in the UK on the 30th December. There would be a press open day on the 2nd January, the exhibition would be open to the public from the 4th January. Online ticket sales for the exhibition were encouraged. After reading that, Marshal ventured in to his concealed basement and rummaged through a chest of drawers to find his press identification badges, which he once wore when he was a police inspector. All Marshal had to do was to blag his way in, on the press open day.

Aaron Loughty telephoned Marshal, and enquired if he would be interested in some part-time detective work. The two agreed a salary; Aaron Loughty asked if Marshal could start straight away and his answer was yes. Marshal could not believe his first assignment; stake-out at Joe Billings Junior's property and notify Aaron Loughty should either Joe or his girlfriend Miss Lewandowski show up at the flat. This concerned Marshal; he suspected that the police might be looking to question them further over the Marzia Bonanno abduction.

It was the next day; Marshal was sat in his car, across the road from the flat, when Chelsea jumped out of a taxi. Chelsea was wheeling a small cabin bag; she had been stopping away somewhere, deduced Marshal. He waited a few minutes then knocked on the front door.

'Oh Marshal, I'm so pleased to see you,' declared Chelsea. 'It's Buster, I haven't heard from him for days, something must have happened.'

Marshal was suddenly aware that Chelsea was extremely distressed. Chelsea invited Marshal into the flat.

She told Marshal, 'Max had been coming in the Megalodon bar where I work. He had been pestering me for private dances. I wouldn't dance for him at first, but he was quite insistent, almost forceful. Buster found out; he asked me how many times had I danced for him. Buster suggested a dozen times, that was a good guess. He hung up on me, threatening to phone Max, threatening to kill him. I've not heard from Buster since.'

Marshal accepted a coffee from Chelsea and decided to phone Max. Marshal agreed with Chelsea, both mobile phones of Buster were out of service.

'Marshal, good to hear from you, is something wrong? Do we have another robbery on the horizon?' asked Max.

'I'm with Chelsea at the moment, she's quite upset, she hasn't heard from Buster in days,' claimed Marshal.

'Oh good, Chelsea's back then,' responded Max.

Marshal thought that was a strange response. 'Tell me Max, what happened on the phone, with you and Buster the other evening?'

Crime is a Killer

'Yes, Buster found out that I had been visiting the Megalodon bar, and that Chelsea kept offering to dance for me,' answered Max. 'He was mad Marshal, cussing and swearing, it took me several minutes to calm him down, but he did eventually.'

'Chelsea kept offering to dance for you, you say,' repeated Marshal. 'How did the discussion finish up?'

Chelsea looked horrified, her eyes opened wide, she shook her head in anguish. Marshal could see by Chelsea's reaction; Max had lied about the dancing.

'I sincerely apologised to Buster, Marshal,' answered Max. 'I promised not to return to the Megalodon and never to see Chelsea again. He seemed to calm down after that.'

'So do you have any idea where Buster might be?' asked Marshal.

'Absolutely no idea Marshal,' claimed Max.

After talking to Max, Marshal explained to Chelsea how he had been hired to inform a private detective, on her or Buster's return to the flat. He warned her that she might soon receive a visit from the police. Try not to give anything away was his advice. Chelsea asked Marshal if he could take her to the lock-up where her and Buster's ransom money was stored away. On entering the lock-up, Chelsea burst into tears. Buster's share of the money was intact; it hadn't been touched. Chelsea stuffed her remaining share into a large holdall bag.

'Something is definitely wrong Marshal,' sobbed Chelsea, 'Buster wouldn't just disappear without any money. He was always complaining about how skint he was.'

'When the police call on you, be sure to report Buster as a missing person,' advised Marshal.

Marshal gave Chelsea a lift back to the flat, then he telephoned Aaron Loughty to notify him of Chelsea's return to Bristol. He told Aaron that Chelsea had been visiting her sister in Manchester.

Max was keen to see Chelsea. She didn't know, but Buster had given him their address. Max took more painkillers, then dressed in some smarter clothes, deciding to visit Chelsea at her home. His wife Eleanor accused him of seeing someone.

When Max arrived, he noticed a police car parked in the street. His eyes glanced toward the front door of Chelsea's flat. Oh my God, thought Max, there was Detective Inspector Blunt, together with another policeman, talking to Chelsea.

Max drove on, he didn't stop. He drove to the Megalodon bar, to drown his sorrows. He also hoped that a beer or two might dull the pain in his aching jaw.

DI Blunt was livid. He so desperately wanted to arrest Joe Billings Junior, instead, he was asked to file a missing person report. The Inspector departed with a portrait photograph of Joe, for his report.

With Christmas fast approaching, Marshal met with Chadd Aitken. Chadd was soon on board with the heist. A bonus being, his boat was moored close to the Great Western Dockyard, in the Floating Harbour, just around the corner from the Mission Hut, claimed Chadd. Marshal decided to contact each member of the Getaway Gang. He suggested to each one, a meeting in the Bedford Arms, on the day after Boxing Day, 27th December. Marshal gave no details away; he just described this forthcoming event as the big one. He referred to it as possibly 'The heist of the decade.'

CHAPTER 19

When Chelsea filed a missing person report with DI Blunt, she provided the Inspector with the timing of her last conversation with Joe Billings Junior. She explained that Joe was intending to speak to someone else after her, Max Currigan. She detailed for the Inspector, Max's visits to the Megalodon bar, his insistence on her dancing for him, and how Joe had found out and was upset. The Inspector quizzed Chelsea on the relationship of Joe and Max. Chelsea played it down somewhat; that they just knew each other from their time in prison together.

DI Blunt and DS Welles visited the home of Max Currigan. His wife, Eleanor, answered the door and explained that Max had set off for work really early that morning.

'Interesting, Mrs Currigan. Max works at the Activity Centre I understand?' enquired DI Blunt.

Eleanor Currigan confirmed Max's place of work and asked, 'What has he done this time?'

'Probably nothing Mrs Currigan, we just want to have a quick word with him about a missing person,' replied DI Blunt. The two officers thanked her and left.

Eleanor wanted to tell the officers that the reason they didn't find any guns the other day, was because Max had concealed them somewhere. Fortunately for Max she held back and stayed silent.

The two officers arrived at the Activity Centre. Max seemed to be the only member of staff working there that morning.

'Good morning Mr Currigan, nice morning for a bonfire,' called out DI Blunt.

Crime is a Killer

DI Blunt was the last person Max wanted to see. It was lucky for Max that he had hidden all the weaponry and ammunition from his house, and had finished burning his clothes and a few cardboard boxes. The incinerator bin was merely smouldering.

'Good morning gents, and what can I do for you this time?' grinned Max.

'Joe Billings Junior, alias Buster, has been reported missing,' declared DI Blunt.

'Done a bunk has he? Ah well, that's Buster for you,' implied Max.

'It appears you were the last person to speak to Mr Billings on the night of,' DI Blunt referred to his pocket notebook once more. 'Why would you meet or speak to Mr Billings, Mr Currigan? When we interviewed you previously, you said prison isn't actually the best place to make friends, yet you are speaking to him. Did you meet with him that night, Mr Currigan?'

'No Inspector,' lied Max, 'Everything was sorted out on the phone.'

'Sorted out Mr Currigan! Did you have a grievance with Mr Billings that might have involved a Miss Lewandowski?' goaded DI Blunt, raising his voice slightly.

Max thought for a moment. The Inspector had obviously been talking to Chelsea, he thought. 'I happened to visit the Megalodon bar where Miss Lewandowski works as a dancer. She came on strong to me. She is a very attractive young lady, Inspector. I couldn't resist taking up her offer to have several dances with her,' lied Max once more. 'I think she must have confessed to Buster; he did phone me that night, he asked me not to visit the bar again.'

'Mr Currigan, when we last spoke, you clearly indicated you do not speak with Mr Billings. How many conversations have you had with him since prison?' questioned DI Blunt.

'Listen Inspector, I didn't call him, he called me,' retaliated Max.

'You both have each other's contact numbers, how come?' quizzed DI Blunt.

'From when we left prison Inspector; we are not friends though,' answered Max.

Changing the subject, DI Blunt made an accusation, 'So where did you move the guns to from your property, Mr Currigan? Did you bring them here?'

'Inspector, let me show you. Follow me,' proposed Max, as he started to walk toward the Activity Centre storeroom.

The officers followed Max into a locked room, full of different rifles.

'Here are some guns,' sneered Max.

At that moment, the first two customers of the day arrived for some clay-pigeon shooting.

'Thank you for showing us the Activity Centre's gun collection.' DI Blunt soon realised that Max Currigan had bluffed and deluded the two officers. 'If it is okay with you Mr Currigan, we might just check with the telephone companies on the frequency of calls you have had with Joe Billings Junior.'

Max thought about that, but he wasn't too concerned; Marshal had organised separate mobile phones for the abduction, which were all destroyed at the time.

Crime is a Killer

During the few days that followed, Marshal and Valesca continued to drive around the country, depositing large sums of used bank notes, until Marshal's share of the ransom money had all been deposited into their joint account.

Missing person posters of Buster had started to arrive in different locations in Bristol and the outlying villages. Posters also appeared on several social media sites.

DI Fishar telephoned DI Blunt, 'Hello Marcel, just a courtesy call to inform you that we are about to arrest Stefan Bonanno as an accessory to the murder of Herman Freud. In an email sent to Otto Natchnebel, there was an instruction provided which read, 'You need to find out why Freud is withholding my stock sale of £195,000.' In a following email it read, 'If F continues to hold onto my money, he will need to disappear.' And in a further email, it read, 'It's time, Otto, for F to vanish.' These emails were sent from Stefan Bonanno's mobile telephone in HMP.'

'My God Gail, the man actually believes he is above the law,' responded DI Blunt. 'Good luck with charging him, and thank you for letting me know.'

'Thank you, Marcel. I have only one question; have you managed to recover any of Stefan Bonanno's half a million pounds?' asked DI Fishar.

There was a pause. 'Sadly no, not a single note has been recovered. It has actually become an embarrassment for the territorial police force. The Chief Constable has called in support from the Flying Squad,' declared DI Blunt.

DS Parkin and DC Jha from the Metropolitan Police paid a visit to Ajay Sawyers home, on behalf of DI Blunt and the Avon and Somerset Police. Ajay explained that he genuinely wanted to buy an old run-down property to renovate, outside of London; Gloucester was compelling. He went on to explain that having found what looked to be the perfect property, they went to the pub to celebrate. Many beers later they decided not to try and drive home, so they broke into the property to spend the night. DS Parkin then challenged Ajay on the pub they visited, that didn't actually exist. Ajay provided another name for a pub, that Niles had conjured up earlier.

'So, tell me exactly, Mr Sawyers, how did you break into the property in question?' asked DS Parkin.

'Dead easy Inspector, we just forced the lock on the back door. It wasn't difficult on such an old neglected property. We simply reset the lock when we left,' claimed Ajay.

Ajay's wife, Brinda, felt uneasy with a further visit of the Metropolitan Police. She warned Ajay that his friend Niles would get him into serious trouble one day.

DS Parkin and DC Jha paid another visit to the home of Niles Easter, only to discover Niles' account of what happened matched Ajay's account, almost word for word.

Marshal telephoned Chelsea; any news on Buster?

'No, nothing Marshal,' replied Chelsea. 'Although the police have started spreading missing person posters around the city.'

'Tell me about it,' responded Marshal. 'That private detective has given me two dozen posters to put up.' Marshal informed Chelsea of the meeting at the Bedford

Crime is a Killer

Arms on the 27th. The heist of the decade, as he described it, without giving out too much information.

'I can't stay in Bristol for Christmas Marshal, unless Buster suddenly turns up. I shall stop with my sister in Manchester. If I'm honest, the kidnapping freaked me out at times Marshal, I'm just not cut out for crime like Buster,' portrayed Chelsea.

DI Blunt received a visit from Detective Chief Inspector Juliet Acklin, from the Flying Squad. DI Blunt spent most of the day briefing the DCI on the abduction of Marzia Bonanno. Her visit that day was timed well, as DCI Acklin was able to sit in on the voice recognition line-up with Marzia. DC Durden operated the recording device; Joe Billings Junior's voice was played fourth, out of five separate voice recordings. They played the clip when Buster was asked if Dillon Kelleher ever talked about Stefan Bonanno. 'Hey if he did, I don't recall, I am useless with names,' said Buster at the time of questioning.

'That's him,' screeched Marzia, 'That's him.'

'Are you certain Marzia?' asked DI Blunt.

'Positive,' responded Marzia, 'I will never forget the night in the bedroom, those words haunt me; 'Not long now honey, the drop is tonight'. Then when I questioned him whether it was my father's money, he said, 'Yes, daddy has put up the cash, we wanted more, but half a million will do for starters.' That aloof tone, standoffish, reticent, sarcastic manner. That's got to be him on that recording.'

'Bingo,' said DI Blunt. 'We have one of the Getaway Gang times two, voice and DNA; now all we need to do is find him.'

'Let's put the four 'police Ps' on the table,' suggested DCI Acklin.

'**Prevent.** Is the gang planning anything else? What major events are coming up in Bristol in the near future?

Pursue. Step up the search for Joe Billings Junior. Airports, ports, Channel Tunnel, social media.

Protect. Is there any more of Stefan Bonanno's family or associates at risk?

Prepare. It might be worth arresting more prison inmates of Joe Billings Junior. Ascertain their weaknesses, impose on those weaknesses.'

Marzia Bonanno was very impressed with DCI Acklin; a woman who means business, she thought.

DI Blunt felt as if he had just had a bulldozer run over him!

27th DECEMBER.

The Getaway Gang met at the Bedford Arms. Marshal was pleased to see his old friend and ex-colleague, landlord Nobby Drummond. Marshal collected Niles Easter from Bath railway station, earlier that day. Marshal welcomed everyone, and introduced Chadd Aitken to the group.

'Chadd was instrumental in helping us to capture Marzia. He executed a diversion for the police, so we could slip Marzia through the roadblock. Chadd also has a boat, but we'll come to that a little later,' set forth Marshal.

The question of Buster came up. Everyone except Niles had seen the missing posters, and calls for sightings, on social media. Marshal looked at Max to capture his facial expression. Max stayed unresponsive; he deliberately didn't make eye contact with Marshal.

Crime is a Killer

'I guess we can't count Buster in on this heist, such a shame,' portrayed Marshal. 'I did ask Chelsea, but she wants out on whatever we were planning. Chelsea has gone to stay with her sister in Manchester, over Christmas.'

Max felt saddened by this announcement, but tried not to show it.

'I have received the first payment from the jewellers heist; £10,000,' announced Marshal. 'That is to be split between the five attendees of the burglary; I propose sending Buster's share to Chelsea, momentarily.'

Marshal then went on to great lengths, to spell out the heist of the decade, as he referred to it.

'This is iconic,' expressed Marshal. 'That such an exhibition should come to Bristol, the urban street art capital of the world. There was a property in Totterdown, on the market, in the region of £300,000. Then suddenly street art was added to it, and people believe its value has increased, three-fold or even more. Simply amazing, the value of world-class street art. I understand there is a work of art sold through a reputable auction house, that's worth over sixteen million pounds; can you imagine that?'

Marshal spent some time talking about the artist Filipe Mar Arrazquito, emphasising that he was certainly in the top ten street artists in the world. He spent time describing the fifteen works of art, with photographs and descriptions. As the articles were passed around the group, everyone was suitably impressed. Marshal touched on the four works of art that had been sold; he slowly read out the names of the buyers, but they didn't mean anything to any of the gang. Marshal indicated the forecast value for each individual artwork ranged from £750,000 to £1.5 million. Many in the group were surprised, some were amazed. Then Marshal read out the painting, 'Sprung from Jail,' was almost certainly purchased by Stefan Bonanno. The room was buzzing with conversations and excitement, until that last name was read out; the room went deathly silent.

It was Connor that commented first, 'Holy smoke Marshal, Stefan Bonanno has bought one; that's just crazy.'

Marshal went on to explain where the art exhibition was to take place, and how easy he thought it would be, to break into the Mission Hut.

'How are you planning to do that Marshal?' asked Yosef.

'JCB,' came his reply. 'I have access to a JCB just up the road, at Ashton Works. I would like to carry out the heist not straight away, when the exhibition gets underway, but maybe the second Sunday, early hours of Monday morning. I would deliver the JCB after the exhibition closes at 4pm on the Sunday. Which brings me to; is there anyone in the group with more JCB experience than I have?'

Donut chipped in, 'I can drive a JCB. I used to work for a construction company, when I lived in Romania.'

'Excellent, you're hired Donut,' confirmed Marshal, who went on to detail the relatively small car park to the rear, leading down to the River Avon. Marshal touched on the central roundabout that the sold artwork would be fixed to.

'I hope to get a good look at how they are fixed, when I attend the press day on the 2nd January.'

'You are going to the press day?' exclaimed Niles.

'Yes, I already have my admission ticket,' replied Marshal. 'For speed, we should have two tool boxes available.'

Donut and Max both raised their arms, volunteering their tool boxes.

Crime is a Killer

'The best way to escape with the paintings, I believe, is by boat, rather than road. By road, we would need either a large van, or truck; it wouldn't take long for the police to set up road blocks in and around Bristol. By boat, we can cruise down the River Avon, up the River Severn, where my lovely re-established girlfriend Valesca,' Marshal stopped to blow Valesca a kiss, 'Has secured a boathouse for us, to conceal the boat and artwork. It's not too far; it's near the Wye estuary, almost perfect in fact. So, with that, I believe Valesca deserves a cut of the riches; any objections anyone?'

The room remained silent, there were no objections.

'That's great, onwards and upwards,' bellowed Marshal. 'Chadd, let's talk a little regarding the boat.'

Chadd passed around a photograph of his river cruiser. 'I currently have it moored at Great Western Dock. I can bring it around to the Mission Hut a few days before the heist, providing there are mooring spaces available nearby. There are just three moorings near the Mission Hut; two are ideal. I aim to keep an eye on the river activity, although this is January, so I don't expect much activity. I have checked; it's high tide at 1.45am on the night Marshal wants to strike. I have also been to have a look at the boathouse with Valesca; it's a good size, very concealed, and it's just up the road, I mean river!'

There was laughter amongst the group.

The gang went on to discuss more details. Niles should stop at Marshal's house. Connor would hire a limo, to collect gang members from their homes and from the boathouse. Two cars would be parked at the boathouse, to bring gang members back to their homes, once the boathouse had been locked and secured.

Finally, Marshal just wanted to hear; was everyone fully on board with the heist.

'Let's go around the room,' suggested Marshal, 'In our out, starting with you Yosef.'

'Well,' answered Yosef, 'This wouldn't generally be my bag, however, this is another opportunity to avenge oneself with Stefan Bonanno, so I'm in.'

They went around the table; no one wanted out. Marshal closed the meeting by providing new mobile telephones to Niles, Yosef and Chadd.

2nd JANUARY.

Marshal arrived at the Mission Hut promptly, for 2pm. Badged as a press officer, he represented the Scarborough Arts Association; he even produced fifty business cards with a false name, address, email and telephone numbers.

The exhibition had a dozen hosts all dressed in blue blazers. The host that latched on to Marshal, introduced himself as Francis. At first, Marshal was amused at his theatrical, effeminate tones, but as the conversation progressed, Marshal discovered that he actually had a welcoming personality, and wicked sense of humour.

Francis enquired about Marshal's background. Marshal went on to tell him how there are some outstanding artists living in north Yorkshire, especially landscape painters. In the town of Scarborough, street art is gaining popularity, which is why his editor had asked him to attend this exhibition in Bristol. Marshal pondered on the fact; he will never go to heaven. Francis was impressed with Marshal's knowledge of Filipe Mar Arrazquito and his artwork. When it came to study the artwork on the central display, Marshal asked Francis,

'Am I right in saying these four works of art have been sold already?'

'Yes, that is correct sir, how wonderful for you to know that,' came the reply.

'Now let me see,' bragged Marshal, pointing at 'Masked Monkey Care'; 'This one has been acquired by someone high-up in the Argentinian health care system. This one,' pointing at 'Dark Money', 'Has been purchased by a Russian businessman. I don't know the other two.'

'That is absolutely astonishing sir,' remarked Francis. 'We were informed 'Creatures Last Tango', the buyer made his wealth in shipping. The 'Sprung from Jail', we were told the buyer remains anonymous.'

'He, or she, is probably in prison!' cracked Marshal.

Both men laughed. It was then, a fair-sized group entered the Mission Hut. Francis made his apologies to Marshal, asking if could help host the new arrivals. Francis pointed out, the artist Filipe Mar Arrazquito and his interpreter might welcome a discussion, with someone so cultured. Marshal was flattered and keen to join the short queue to talk to the artist, but first, this was his big chance to study the central display.

Each work of art was joined to a wooden frame at the rear of the canvas. On each side there were three heavy bolts, securing it to a metal central framework. Not insuperable to dismantle post-haste, thought Marshal. He studied the laser beam sensors, one in each corner of the hut. That would be the most far-reaching difficulty to overcome; the local police stations alerted by alarms.

THE HEIST.

Chadd brought his boat up the River Avon, to moor close to the Mission Hut, two days before the heist was due to take place. His mooring location was ideal. Donut arrived just after 5pm on the JCB. He parked the vehicle behind the Mission Hut. This manoeuvre remained unnoticed by any neighbours or passers-by.

Connor, alias Sean McBurney, hired a seven-seater BMW from a dealership in Chepstow. The intention was to leave the vehicle at the Mission Hut, and notify the dealership after the heist. Yosef and Donut had their vehicles parked at the boathouse.

It was 1.30am, Donut started up the JCB and drove it hard into the back wall of the hut. There was an almighty crack.

'Push harder Donut,' suggested Marshal.

Donut drove hard into the back wall again; there was a second loud crack. His third impact split the galvanised steel wall from top to bottom. Donut pushed once more, to create an opening wide enough for human entry.

'Good work, Donut,' roared Marshal, 'Now let's park that monster, and let's get moving with the heist.'

Each man had their task prepared. Connor and Chadd climbed inside the metal framework to clasp the nuts, while Donut and Max power-loosened the bolts. The first canvas released was carried down to the boat by Niles. The second canvas, carried down by Marshal and Yosef. The third, by Max and Chadd. The final canvas was carried by Donut and Connor. All four works of art were safely on board the boat. Chadd started the engine; Connor loosened the mooring ropes and jumped onboard. Chadd's boat purred off the mooring space, and down the River Avon.

As the Gang broke the laser beam sensors at the Mission Hut, alarms were activated in Bridewell Street, Trinity Road, and Broadbury Road police stations. A unit from Bridewell police station were the first to arrive; disconcerted by the damage to the Mission Hut, and no sign of any marauders remaining at the scene, the unit radioed back to HQ for more assistance. A local neighbour appeared at the location, claiming that the intruders had got away by boat.

Chadd was driving the boat very carefully in the dark of the night. Stood by his side was Max, with a loaded sawed-off shotgun. As the boat approached the Clifton Suspension Bridge, Chadd commented on how haunting that bridge looked, perched on top of the gorge, with the moon overhead. Just before the bridge was the landing strip, on the Hotwell Road.

'This is where you are jumping off, I believe, Marshal,' called out Chadd.

Chadd manoeuvred the boat to pull alongside the landing jetty. Marshal and Valesca climbed off the boat. Not far away was a climb of steep steps leading up to Clifton, walking distance from Marshal's house. Niles was due to stay at Marshal's home that night.

'Are you jumping off too Niles?' called Marshal.

'You go ahead Marshal, and do what you need to do,' replied Niles, 'That looks too big a climb for me. I'll give the guys a hand to unload the artwork when we get to the boathouse. I can scrounge a lift back to Clifton.'

'Okay, be careful at the boathouse everyone,' forewarned Marshal. 'You had better get going Chadd.'

Marshal and Chadd slapped hands together. Chadd steered the boat away from the landing strip and continued down the River Avon.

As they approached the River Avon estuary to join the River Severn, they could see vehicle headlights high in the air, from the M5 motorway bridge.

'Look at that traffic Max, it's 2.30 in the morning, there's quite a few vehicles on that motorway,' stated Chadd.

'Yes, it's a great time for HGVs to travel,' responded Max.'

It was then that the night air echoed with the sound of gunfire. Six shots could be heard. Chadd slumped down over the steering wheel, and leant on the accelerator lever. Max fired his shotgun aimlessly in the air; a bullet had pierced the side of his head. There were another six rounds fired. Niles was stood at the back of the boat; with his large frame, he suffered two bullets to his chest; he fell backwards into the river. Yosef, Donut and Connor scrambled down inside the boat. Connor had been hit in the top of the arm; he was screaming. The boat accelerated into a boatyard, immediately before the bridge. It crashed hard into a wooden jetty, supported by scaffolding poles. One of the poles fractured and wrecked the hull of the boat, which started to break up on impact. What followed was a fire, then a very loud explosion. Boat debris, bodies, body parts and extremely damaged artwork littered the river. No one could have possibly survived that.

But who fired the shots? Who was the marksman? Was it the Flying Squad? Or was it a hired gunman? If it was the latter, who would sanction a hit-man? Stefan Bonanno?

CHAPTER 20

At first light that morning, there were at least two dozen police officers at the scene. Frogmen, forensics, Flying Squad, Avon and Somerset Crime Investigation, even collision scene management were in attendance.

DI Blunt and DCS Dawes-Drake were both given early morning calls by the front desk at Bridewell police station. DI Blunt and DCS Dawes-Drake arrived at the scene simultaneously. They were both surprised to see DCI Acklin of the Flying Squad, had arrived ahead of them.

The two officers sidled over to the DCI.

'Good morning Ma'am, I see you had your early morning call too,' announced DCS Dawes-Drake.

'Good morning gentlemen. Yes, I wouldn't have missed this for all the world,' responded DCI Acklin. 'A marksman on the river bank seems to have shot a few of the villains from this morning's street art robbery. Farcical as it seems, all this mud along the River Avon, and the boat happened to plough into a scaffolding pole in this boatyard. A preposterous stroke of luck for us.'

Frogmen had already pulled two bodies out of the river; Max Currigan and Chadd Aitken. They were laid out on the grass knoll on the edge of the riverbank. DI Blunt inspected both corpses; one body he recognised instantly; it was Max Currigan. The other body he didn't recognise.

'Here is his wallet,' DCI Acklin held up a forensic polythene bag. 'His name is Chadd Aitken.'

'Well,' spluttered DI Blunt, 'Max Currigan is one of the prison inmates we were close on the tail of. Perhaps the other gent is merely the boat driver.'

Frogmen had managed to position a stretcher under the body of Niles Easter. He was still alive, but unconscious. An ambulance had parked up on nearby waste ground, ready to take Niles to the hospital. It took four men to carry the stretcher. DI Blunt inspected the body and confirmed it was Niles Easter. Sadly, Niles died in the ambulance.

DCI Acklin approached DCS Dawes-Drake and DI Blunt.

'Divers and forensic officers have been instructed to position any other body-parts taken from the river, onto those large plastic sheets, under the bridge,' declared DCI Acklin. 'There are several vehicles on their way from London. We will salvage whatever we can, to transfer to the Metropolitan Police Forensic Science Laboratory on the Lambeth Road. To our advantage, low tide is expected at 8.10am.'

'But Ma'am, we can manage the forensic duties here in Bristol,' proposed DI Blunt.

'Sorry Marcel, this is a case for the Flying Squad now; we will be overseeing the rest of the investigation,' confirmed DCI Acklin.

At that moment, Alfonso Dacosta arrived on foot. Alfonso was the exhibition's main organiser. He was extremely distressed when he reached the three police officers on the side of the river bank.

'The paintings,' cried Alfonso. 'The paintings, are they safe?'

'Not so,' assured DCI Acklin, 'They have been blown to smithereens.'

Crime is a Killer

Alfonso Dacosta explained to the officers who he was. He elucidated that the four works of art that had been stolen happened to be the only paintings that Filipe Mar Arrazquito had sold.

'Were they insured?' asked DCS Dawes-Drake.

Alfonso Dacosta shrugged his shoulders. He explained the Mission Hut had liability insurance, but as for the owners, he wasn't sure. Alfonso took a piece of paper from his jacket pocket. On it, was the names of the buyers. Stefan Bonanno was the last name read; the three officers looked at each other in astonishment.

Marshal had set the alarm for 6.30am, despite being up half of the night, orchestrating the heist of the decade. He made himself a fruit and yoghurt breakfast, and wondered why Niles hadn't showed up. Maybe he had slept at one of the other gang members', he thought. Marshal switched on the morning television, local news channel. Local TV cameras and reporters were already located in close proximity to the fatal accident, on the River Avon. Marshal was aghast, thunderstruck; he ran into the bedroom to wake Valesca, with the horrific news. They both sat and watched the reporting of the incident, in silence, in disbelief, in incredulity.

'Valesca, you need to gather your things and head out of here as soon as possible. The police do not know you were involved,' uttered Marshal. He kissed his girlfriend on the head. 'You know what to do.'

Valesca was scared; she never spoke, she just smiled at Marshal and nodded her head. The pair gathered their belongings; Valesca returned home to her apartment. They both had new mobile phones to communicate to each other. Marshal already had a suitcase and cabin bag packed; he had a flight to New York booked for later that day.

By dusk that day, all of the body parts, critical debris and partial remains of any artwork, had all been salvaged from the river. Both the Flying Squad and the Avon and Somerset Police were keen to find out whether Joe Billings Junior was on that boat.

Marshal drove his car into a rented garage in Clifton. He took a taxi to Bristol Temple Meads station, caught a train to London Paddington, then boarded the Heathrow Express to reach the airport. Marshal became very nervous, timorous, when he departed through the airport security. He was not confronted, much to his relief. He boarded the airplane and flew to New York. A seven-night stay was planned.

The following morning, DCS Dawes-Drake took a call from DCI Acklin.

'Good morning Elliott. The Met's forensic team, through bank cards and driving licences on the bodies recovered from the River Avon, have identified three of the bodies. A Yosef Villin, a Connor Jackson and a Lonut Coltescu, who had a Romanian driving licence.'

'No identification on Joe Billings Junior, or Dillon Kelleher?' questioned DCS Dawes Drake.

'No Elliott,' answered DCI Acklin. 'Either they weren't on the boat, or we may have to dredge the river one more time, to make sure we haven't missed anything.'

Crime is a Killer

'I can confirm, those three names were all prison inmates together, that formed part of the Getaway Gang,' established DCS Dawes-Drake. 'DI Blunt is making a house call on Chadd Aitken, as we speak. A DS Parkin of the Met has agreed to make a house call on Niles Easter.'

'Excellent Elliott, we will try and organise one more search of the river tomorrow,' proposed DCI Acklin.

Marshal had planned for his week in New York, some sightseeing, a theatre, but he had singled out three casinos to visit. One in Queens, one in Brooklyn and one on Long Island. Valesca had agreed to lay low, stay at her apartment in the city, and return to work as if nothing had happened.

Chelsea had seen the catastrophe on national television. Six men were declared killed in the shooting and accident, on the evening news. She recognised five names; she didn't recognise Chadd Aitken. How horrible, she thought; but where the hell was Buster? He wouldn't have given up the opportunity to be involved in that robbery. But it doesn't sound as if he was on that boat either; where is Buster, angered Chelsea. She stopped to think; what about Marshal? There was no mention of Marshal. She tried ringing him; his mobile telephone was out of service.

DI Blunt's team had their work cut out that day, notifying the families of the deceased.

Stefan Bonanno's eldest daughter Vittoria visited him in HMP.

'Hello papa, how are you,' gently asked Vittoria.

'Better for seeing you my little Gioia. Any news on the painting?' asked Stefan.

'I have spoken to the police, and they tell me all four of the paintings stolen from the art exhibition were totally destroyed,' came her answer.

Stefan Bonanno's eyes glazed over. He had not had the opportunity to insure his newly acquired work of art.

'Did you see the names of the men that the police have announced were on that boat?' asked his daughter.

'I did my little Gioia.' Stefan Bonanno just shook his head.

Aaron Loughty was assigned the task of watching intermittently, Joe Billings Junior's flat, and Dillon Kelleher's property. He confirmed to DI Blunt that he was unable to make contact with Dillon; his mobile was out of service.

Connor's father was distraught. He tried to be strict with Connor at times; Connor had done some stupid, imprudent things with cars in the past; nevertheless, he loved his son just the same. His eyes filled. Mr Jackson went to his son's bedroom, in search of Connor's vehicle log book. He decided he would sell Connor's car. Just looking at it parked on the road would be a constant reminder of the execrable side of his son's personality.

Police divers spent that day dredging the location of the fatal accident, upstream and downstream, looking for more evidence. More items were recovered from the mud of the River Avon, but nothing that would assist their enquiries significantly. There was still no sign of anything belonging to Joe Billings Junior or Dillon Kelleher.

Chelsea returned with her sister Morgan, to Bristol. She had a very quick look around the flat. There was no sign that

Crime is a Killer

Buster had been back to the flat. Morgan drove to Chelsea and Buster's lock up. There was still no sign of Buster being there either. This is crazy, thought Chelsea; she picked up Buster's share of the ransom, and the two sisters returned to Manchester with Buster's pickings.

Marshal's week in New York soon came to an end. He was sat in the airport waiting for a flight to take him on to Rio de Janeiro, in Brazil. He had time to ring Valesca, although he was conscious of the cost of an international mobile phone call. They discussed the possible house clearance at Marshal's house, once the police activity had died down. They touched on Connor's share of the ransom money.

'In my concealed basement, there must be £50,000 remaining, of used bank notes, that belonged to Connor. We can't give it to his family; it would incriminate me to the kidnapping. We should try and bank it; are you okay with that darling?' asked Marshal.

'£50,000, yes I'm very okay with banking that,' replied Valesca.

Marshal laughed. 'Any money received from now on, from the jewellery heist, we shall have to bank. The exception being Buster's share, which I can still send on to Chelsea for the time being. When it comes to returning to my house, be careful darling, and keep a look out for that private detective and his black Mercedes.'

Chelsea checked her bank account on her mobile phone. Someone had deposited £2,000. She verified the details; it was from Marshal. He must be still alive, thought Chelsea.

DC Durden added Rishi Bhand and Morgan Bhand to one of the storyboards, next to Chelsea Lewandowski. She telephoned DI Blunt.

'Boss, Chelsea had one sister, Morgan. She married a Rishi Bhand; they live in Salford, Manchester. I have their address; I just need to trace a contact number for Morgan.'

DI Blunt welcomed this latest development. He was not only looking for a missing person in Joe Billings Junior, but now he needed to locate Dillon Kelleher and Chelsea Lewandowski.

Marshal fell in love with Rio de Janeiro. He had booked a ten-night stay in the city. Marshal had half a dozen cheap watches with him; he was advised that should he get mugged, he should just hand over his watch, in order to save his own skin. During his stay there, he visited Copacabana Beach, Ipanema Beach and the absolutely amazing thirty-eight metre Christ the Redeemer statue, at the top of Mount Corcovado. Marshal's favourite sightseeing adventure was taking the cable car to Sugarloaf Mountain. He also visited the Grand Casino Iguazu Resort on several occasions; he figured he was $200 up from his gambling escapades in New York. Walking back to his hotel from the casino most nights, he capitulated two watches.

Yosef's wife, Leah, made a decision to downsize their property in Bristol. Without Yosef, there was no need for a six-bedroom property to accommodate Yosef's guests. Nor did she need to live close to, and overlook, Woodlands Golf and Country Club. She had seen a four-bedroom house with manageable gardens in Clifton that she really liked. The three children were not so keen on the upheaval, but they all agreed, it was prudent to retrench.

Lonut Coltescu's partner, Alexandru, hated not having Lonut around. Hated that he would never ever see him again. Alexandru decided to quit his job at the demolition company, and return to Transylvania. He would try and re-establish his relationship with Patrin. Lonut's and Alexandru's share of the kidnapping money remained intact in Patrin's locked caravan, on site. Alexandru would have to find a way to transfer that cash to Romania.

DCS Dawes-Drake received an international telephone call; it was from a Comisario Inspector, Santiago Bianchi, of the Policia Federal Argentina. His position translated as an equivalent rank to Superintendent Inspector. CI Bianchi wanted to hear the details, first hand, of the Filipe Mar Arrazquito heist in Bristol. After DCS Dawes-Drake had finished apprising CI Bianchi with the chain of events, CI Bianchi made a claim that shocked the DCS. He considered the Bristol heist to be secondary, in the Argentinian art world, to the Bellas Artes national museum in 1980. He went on to explain in that robbery, sixteen masterpieces were stolen, including works by Cezanne, Degas, Matisse, and the most famous of all, 'Portrait of a Woman', by Renoir. The DCS put down the phone, puffed out his cheeks, and sat in silence for several minutes afterwards.

DI Blunt, DS Welles and private detective Aaron Loughty were present at the funeral of Chadd Aitken. The police had discovered the link to the road-block deviation on the night of Marzia Bonanno's abduction. They also attended the funerals of Yosef Villin, Max Currigan, Connor Jackson and even Niles Easter, in north London. Lonut Coltescu's family wanted his bodily remains returned to Romania. The officers were not really there to pay their respects, they were on the lookout for Billings and Kelleher. Aaron

Loughty was given the task of searching the grounds of the different cemeteries and crematoriums, just in case the two ex-prisoners showed their faces, from a distance. Neither men were seen at the funerals, which DI Blunt found frustrating.

At the end of Marshal's stay in Rio, he bought a jeep to travel on to his next destination, the island of Ilha Grande, off the Costa Verde coastline. He arrived at the town of Angra dos Reis, where he took a ferry ride over to the Island. On the island, Marshal was in awe of the beautiful beaches, scattered along the route to his hired villa. Marshal had a map on how to find beach house Abacaxi close to Dios Rios beach. It was explained to him, Abacaxi would translate as pineapple. When Marshal reached the house, he could understand the name; there in the front garden, stood six magnificent pineapple trees. This was going to be one hell of an adventure, thought Marshal. He had taken out a six-month rental on the beach house.

One month had passed since the boat catastrophe; Valesca considered that the interest in movements at Marshal's property had cooled off. She organised a house clearance, which went seemingly unnoticed. She did keep a few of Marshal's ornaments and artwork, for her apartment in the city centre. Valesca found an estate agent that promised to sell the property in Clifton, without advertisement or promotion, no information on social media at all, and no property specification brochure; it was to be sold purely by accompanied viewing.

Crime is a Killer

Chelsea used hers' and Buster's ransom funds to put a deposit down on an apartment in Salford. She managed to find work in a departmental store, as a make-up consultant.

Chelsea was re-arrested by DI Blunt, and put under pressure to revisit the night of the abduction. To their advantage, the police were able to unnerve Chelsea with the facts that Buster's DNA had matched hairs in a black wig recovered from the Liberty Club. In addition, Marzia Bonanno had identified Buster's voice in a police audio line-up. Chelsea admitted to making one phone call in the Liberty Club that night, together with purchasing certain clothing for Marzia whilst Marzia was held captive by the gang. Chelsea was charged; her brother-in-law Rishi, put up bail for her. Chelsea's court case was announced for the following October.

Marshal was loving life on the island of Ilha Grande. His favourite beach bar was Domingo's Palacio. Interpreted as God's Palace. Marshal made a good friend in bar manager Didi. Didi arranged Portuguese lessons for Marshal, and helped him cultivate the grounds at the beach house. Once Marshal got to know Didi well, there was the occasional drink, sometimes a meal, on the house. Didi once organised a mini-bus to Rio, on a casino trip; Marshal was one of the first to be invited. Life was good for Marshal.

Max's wife Eleanor found romance again; a work colleague from the office where she worked. She knew of her co-worker's affection for her, but Eleanor always stayed loyal to Max, although she often wondered why.

Marshal's house in Clifton had a buyer. The family were from the Lebanon; the new owner was a diplomat, forced to flee from Beirut with his family. The secrecy of the property purchase was an ideal situation for the asylum-seeking family. Once sold, Valesca would give notice to her employer and fly to Miami, to team up with Marshal again.

Avon and Somerset Police organised a wider search of the greater Bristol area, looking to try and find any evidence that might lead to the whereabouts of Joe Billings Junior. Footpaths, parks, woodland, lakes, waste ground, tributary rivers and streams were searched, to no avail. There were no records of Billings leaving the country. The police were able to establish however, that Dillon Kelleher had flown to New York, the day after the River Avon tragedy. They were also able to establish that he had flown on to Rio de Janeiro, one week later.

Valesca arrived in Miami with double her airline allowance of luggage. Marshal was at the airport to meet her. Valesca had instructed Marshal to travel light, so he could take responsibility for half of her baggage, when they flew on to Brazil. Florida seemed like a honeymoon for Marshal and Valesca. They packed in a great deal of sight-seeing; Cape Canaveral, Cocoa Beach; the couple tried their luck with surfing and Segway transportation. They visited Disney, with a three-day pass to Magic Kingdom, Hollywood Studios and Epcot. They finished their stay on the Mexican Gulf coastline, at the idyllic town of Destin. The couple agreed, a ten-day vacation in Florida was far too short; they would have to return.

When Marshal and Valesca arrived at Rio airport, they noticed what seemed like extra police and sniffer dogs.

Crime is a Killer

Marshal noticed a wanted poster, with the name Dillon Kelleher on it. How did he get through customs he asked himself? He did have a new passport, and the photograph on the poster was from when he was in prison. He had grown his hair since then. He put sunglasses on and stayed close to Valesca; he figured the police might not be looking for a couple. They went straight to Marshal's jeep in the long-stay car park. Marshal had booked a motel room to show Valesca the beauty of Rio; he decided to cancel the room and drive straight to his hired beach house at Dios Rios. On arrival, Valesca fell in love with the beach house, and its location.

'We can stay here as long as you like darling,' conveyed Marshal, 'We should be safe here, and amongst friends.' He was referring to Didi and the guys at Domingo's Palacio.

The October soon came around; it was time for Chelsea Lewandowski's court case. Seven males and five females formed the jury. Chelsea was always considered an accessory to the crimes she had been charged with throughout the trial. She denied taking any of the ransom money. When questioned, she declared that Joe Billings Junior had a share of the money, but to that day she had no idea where Joe was, or where he had stashed his money. When questioned if Chelsea had been given any of the pilfered cash, stolen by Joe Billings Junior, she admitted to a spending spree of £1,500 in Manchester. She believed that would help her cause. Chelsea was also questioned on how she had arrived with the deposit for her new apartment in Manchester. Chelsea claimed she had saved that amount of money from dancing at the Megalodon bar, in Bristol.

DI Blunt made an appearance in the witness box. He was questioned on the whereabouts of Joe Billings Junior. The Inspector detailed the extensive searches for the wanted criminal, however, DI Blunt confirmed that Avon and Somerset Police had temporarily closed the case, which was now in the hands of the ICMP, International Commission on Missing Persons, and in support, the NCIC, National Crime Information Centre.

Chelsea's barrister's closing statement was, 'One wonders whether this Billings character and his money will ever be seen again, my Lord!'

The trial had come to a close; the jury re-entered the courtroom, followed by the Judge, 'All rise,' was called. Chelsea was traumatised, shaking with fear.

The Judge addressed the Presiding Juror, 'Has the jury reached a verdict on the charge of false imprisonment involving unlawful and intentional, or reckless detention of Marzia Bonanno against her will?'

'We have your honour,' replied the Foreperson, 'Not guilty.'

Chelsea thought she was going to faint, but she held it together for the next verdict.

Addressing the Presiding Juror once more the Judge asked, 'Has the jury reached a verdict on the charge of dishonest taking of property belonging to Stefan Bonanno, with the intention of permanently depriving him of that property?'

'We have your honour,' announced the Foreperson, 'Not guilty.'

Chelsea closed her eyes in absolute relief.

'And finally,' enquired the Judge, 'Has the jury reached a verdict on the charge of perverting the course of justice?'

Crime is a Killer

'We have your honour,' confirmed the Foreperson, 'Guilty.'

Chelsea looked shocked, horrified; she turned to her barrister, who gestured for her to stay calm.

The Judge sentenced Chelsea to a two-year suspended sentence and ordered her to pay £10,000 bail, which her brother-in-law Rishi offered to cover, and to repay the £1,500 dishonestly consumed. The Judge considered two counts of not guilty in her favour; he also considered that both Joe Billings Junior and Dillon Kelleher used coercive and controlling behaviour towards Miss Lewandowski at the time of the abduction.

Marshal and Valesca were having a fun-loving, relaxing time at Dios Rios Beach. Four months on from Valesca arriving in Brazil, Didi organised a coach trip into Rio de Janeiro. They visited the main sights, and had a magnificent day. Marshal was pleased not to see a single wanted poster of himself. Perhaps the search for him had started to become less intense, he thought. Valesca communicated quite well that day; her use of the Portuguese language was almost as good as Marshal's.

Months later, Marshal was sat on a sun lounger drinking a cocktail, outside the beach house. Valesca was inside the house preparing lunch. A Brazilian police truck arrived at the house. Four officers jumped out of the vehicle and ran over to Marshal. Marshal looked startled to see them. The officers tipped up his sun lounger, laid Marshal on his stomach, and handcuffed him behind his back. Marshal struggled, but the officers without haste bundled Marshal into the truck, and drove off. Valesca saw the officers dragging Marshal off, and into the truck. She screamed for them to stop, but it was too late.

The Brazilian police drove Marshal to the station of the Civil Police in Rio, where he was introduced to three officers of the Policia Federal Argentina. There was an exchange; the Argentine police took Marshal away in their police wagon. Only one of the officers spoke some broken English. Marshal recognised 'Stealing Filipe Mar Arrazquito paintings.' Marshal knew then that he had been caught for the Mission Hut heist in Bristol. Marshal was gutted.

The Argentine police notified the British Embassy in Buenos Aires, of Dillon Kelleher's capture and imprisonment. In turn, the Embassy made contact with London. The Flying Squad put pressure on the UK Government to extradite Dillon Kelleher, to be prosecuted in the UK, as the crime took place in the country's jurisdiction. The Argentinian Embassy and police were unresponsive, on many occasions. Valesca flew from Rio de Janeiro to Buenos Aires, to visit the local police with an Embassy agent. Sadly, her efforts to find Marshal proved unsuccessful. The Argentinian authorities would not even disclose which prison Marshal was held in; it was confidential, they claimed.

Two months later, Valesca returned to England. She closed down the joint bank account, and transferred the money to her own account. This all went under the radar of the UK police. She wondered if she would ever see Marshal again.

The body of Buster Billings was never found.

Marzia Bonanno sought psychological help in the months that followed her terrifying ordeal. Marzia did perform again despite the tribulations of the abduction. The Goddess of Rock band performed two Christmas shows that year, in London and in Hamburg. It was as if Marzia had never left the rock scene, she was pulsating, seductive and alluring once more.

Chadd Aitken was murdered, before his driving convictions for the Marzia Bonanno abduction came to trial. The police only discovered the link, in due course.

Stefan Bonanno was sentenced in a Crown Court for third-degree murder of Herman Freud. Guilty of perpetrating the murder, without any design to effect death. A sentence of twenty years' imprisonment was to be added to his existing term. Stefan would appeal against the sentencing. Many people wondered whether Stefan would spend his last days in HMP.

Otto Natchnebel, whilst waiting for his trial, had both legs badly smashed in his prison cell. Whereas Stefan Bonanno's trial went ahead, Otto's trial was postponed, whilst he learnt to walk again.

The marksman was never divulged; no one ever confessed to the execution of those six men on the boat.

Marshal died in a prison cell in Argentina. The British Embassy, and in turn, the London Embassy, the Flying Squad, and the Avon and Somerset Police, were notified of his death. Despite numerous attempts to reclaim Marshal's corpse, it remained in Argentina, at an undisclosed location. Marshal was only thirty-seven.

Barry Hillier

ACKNOWLEDGEMENTS

I would like to start with a big thank you to my wife Sue. I like to write mostly in the late afternoon, or early evening. Sue would ask, 'What time would you like dinner?'

We would agree a time, and I would carry on writing.

From the kitchen I would hear, 'Ten minutes.' On a few occasions I would hear, 'Dishing up. It's on the plate.'

Sue really enjoyed my second novel; it certainly helped to pass the time for us both, throughout lockdown.

I must once again, thank my daughter Kirstie and my son-in-law Gary. Despite working full time throughout the lockdown, and taking home tutoring to Ella (7) and Isabel (3), they found the time to read each up-to-date chapter. What I found really encouraging, was their enthusiasm and passion toward the story as it developed.

A big thank you to Claire Walton for creating the book cover. Claire's avant-garde approach I love. On first draft, all the family were very complimentary of Claire's cover design. I thought, it followed the 'Nightmares' cover, with a striking likeness. A signature design in the making.

I must say a big thank you to Mike Thompson. Mike has this amazing ability to interrogate novels. The story, the characters, facts, places, links to features used earlier in the book. I refer to Mike's contribution, as sanity checking, I really appreciate his astute observations and judgement.

A final thank you must go to my gym buddy, Derek Stevens. His idea of a bent copper in the prison community, not only changed the course of the story, it was the foundation for **Crime is a Killer**.

Crime is a Killer

Also available by author *Barry Hillier*

Nightmares at Ye Olde Elm Tree

A gripping, supernatural thriller. When did the nightmares begin at Ye Olde Elm Tree? Was it when landlord Albert Baines died tragically? Or was it before? Or was it a long time ago? Three salesmen planned an overnight stop at a quintessential, three-hundred, year old public house and Inn. Did the nightmares really start when they drove into the car park of Ye Olde Elm Tree?

If only the Devons family had not sought revenge on landlady Annie Baines, the nightmares may not have continued so forcefully. If only the local police could have incriminated someone, something, from the spirit world.

Barry Hillier

Printed in Great Britain
by Amazon

71270356R00132